A TREASURY OF STORIES
FOR
FIVE
YEAR OLDS

Kingfisher Books, Grisewood & Dempsey Ltd,
Elsley House, 24–30 Great Titchfield Street,
London W1P 7AD

First published in hardcover in 1989 by Kingfisher Books
First published in paperback in 1991 by Kingfisher Books

10 9 8 7

BRITISH LIBRARY CATALOGUING IN PUBLICATION DATA
Treasury of stories for five year olds.
1. Children's short stories in English to 1985. Anthologies
I. Blishen, Edward, 1920– II. Blishen, Nancy
III. Noakes, Polly
823'.01'089282
ISBN 0 86272 806 1

Designed by Penny Mills
Phototypeset by Waveney Typesetters, Norwich
Printed in Spain by Graficas Reunidas, Madrid

A TREASURY OF STORIES FOR FIVE YEAR OLDS

Chosen by

EDWARD & NANCY BLISHEN

Illustrated by

POLLY NOAKES

Kingfisher Books

CONTENTS

THE RARE SPOTTED BIRTHDAY PARTY

Margaret Mahy

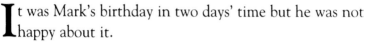

It was Mark's birthday in two days' time but he was not happy about it.

His mother had made a wonderful cake, round, brown and full of nuts and raisins and cherries. There were balloons and party hats hidden in the high cupboard with the Christmas decorations and old picture books. But Mark was not happy.

It was his birthday in two days' time and he had the measles.

Everyone was getting the measles.

"Measles are going around," said Mark's little sister Sarah.

John with the sticking-out ears had the measles.

The twins next door – James and Gerald – had the measles. They had the same brown hair, the same brown eyes, and now they both had the same brown spots.

Mark's friend, Mousey, had the measles. Mousey had so many freckles everyone was surprised that measles could find any room on him.

"Mousey must be even more spotted than I am," said Mark.

"Mousey must be more spotted than *anyone*," Sarah said. "He is a rare spotted mouse."

"It's worse for me," said Mark. "No one can have a birthday when they are covered in spots."

"No one would be able to come," said Sarah. "Do you feel sick, Mark?"

"I feel a bit sick," said Mark. "Even if I *could* have a birthday, I don't think I would want it."

"That is the worst thing," said Sarah. "Not even *wanting* a birthday is worst of all."

Two days later, when the birthday really came, Mark did not feel sick any more. He just felt spotty.

He opened his presents at breakfast.

His mother and father had given him a camera. It was small, but it would take real pictures. Sarah gave him a paint box. (She always gave him a paint box. Whenever Mark got a new paint box, he gave Sarah the old one.)

All morning they painted.

"It feels funny today," said Mark. "It doesn't feel like a birthday. It doesn't feel special at all."

Sarah had painted a class of children. Now she began to paint spots on them.

Lunch was plain and healthy.

In the afternoon Mark's mother started to brush him all over. She brushed his hair. She brushed his dressing-gown, though it was new and did not need brushing. She brushed his slippers.

"We will have a birthday drive," she said. "The car windows will stop the measles from getting out."

They drove out into the country and up a hill that

Mark knew. "There's Peter's house," he said. "Peter-up-the-hill! He has measles, too."

"We might pay him a visit for a moment," Mark's mother said. "He won't catch measles from you if he has them already."

The front door was open. They rang the bell and walked in. Then Mark got a real surprise! The room was full of people. Lots of the people were boys wearing dressing-gowns – all of them spotty boys, MEASLE-Y boys.

"Happy birthday! Happy birthday!" they shouted.

There was John with the sticking-out ears. His ears were still a bit spotty around the edges. There were the twins, James and Gerald. Measles made them look more like each other than ever before. There was Mousey. You could not tell where his freckles left off and his measles began. There was Peter-up-the-hill in a pink dressing-gown, and Peter-next-to-the-shop in a bluey-green one.

"Happy birthday! Happy birthday!" they all shouted.

"It's a measle party," Mark's mother explained. "So many people are getting over measles we decided to have a measle party on your birthday."

"Have you brought my birthday cake?" asked Mark.

"It is in a tin box in the back of the car," said his mother. "I would not forget an important thing like that."

What a funny, spotty, measle-y party! All the guests except Sarah were wearing dressing-gowns.

They played a game called 'Painting Spots on an Elephant'. They played 'Measle-y Chairs' (this is like 'Musical Chairs' except that people who play it have to have the measles).

Sarah found a piece of blue chalk and drew spots all over her face. "I've got *blue* measles," she said.

12

"Mine are very unusual spots." (She did not like being the only person without any spots at all.)

Then came the party food. They had spaghetti and meat balls. They had fruit salad and ice cream, and glasses of orange juice. The fruit salad had strawberries and grapes in it.

Then Mark's mother brought in the cake she had made. It was iced with white icing, and it was spotted and dotted and spattered with pink dots.

"Measles!" cried Mark. "The cake's got measles!" He thought it was the funniest, nicest cake he had ever seen. The measles made it taste extremely delicious.

A measle cake for a measle party! A spotty cake for a dotty party!

"I don't think I'll have a piece of cake," said Sarah. "I don't feel very well . . . I feel all hot and cross."

"Heigh-ho!" said Mark's mother. "I think I know what is wrong."

"You are probably getting the measles," said Mark. "Perhaps *you* will have a measle party too."

"We will think of something else for Sarah," said his mother. "But now we must go home."

"Can't I have a measle party as well?" Sarah pleaded. "I want one, too."

"Measle parties are like comets," said Mark's mother. "If you see one in twenty years you are lucky."

She took Mark and Sarah home, with Mark thinking to himself that it was worth getting the measles at birthday time if a special measles party was the result.

After all, not many people have been to one.

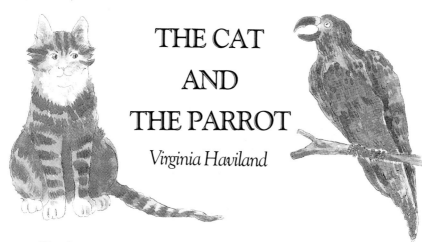

THE CAT
AND
THE PARROT

Virginia Haviland

O nce upon a time a cat and a parrot agreed to ask each other to dinner in turn. First the cat would ask the parrot, then the parrot would invite the cat, and so on.

The cat in his turn was so stingy that he provided nothing for dinner but a pint of milk, a small slice of fish, and a bit of rice – which the parrot had to cook himself! He was too polite to complain, but he did not find it a good meal.

When it was the parrot's turn to entertain the cat, he cooked a great dinner, and did it before his guest arrived. Most tempting of all he offered was a clothes-basketful of crisp, brown cakes. He put four hundred and ninety-eight spicy cakes before the cat, and kept only two for himself.

Well, the cat ate every bit of the good food prepared by the parrot and began on the pile of cakes. He ate the four hundred and ninety-eight, then asked for more.

"Here are my two cakes," said the parrot. "You may eat them."

The cat ate the two cakes. He then looked around and asked for still more.

"Well," said the parrot, "I don't see anything more, unless you wish to eat me!"

The cat showed no shame. Slip! Slop! Down his throat went the parrot!

An old woman who happened to be near saw all this and threw a stone at the cat. "How dreadful to eat your friend the parrot!"

"Parrot, indeed!" said the cat. "What's a parrot? I've a great mind to eat you, too." And before you could say a word, slip! slop! down went the old woman!

The cat started down the road, feeling fine. Soon he met a man driving a donkey. When the man saw the cat he said, "Run away, cat, or my donkey might kick you to death."

"Donkey, indeed!" said the cat. "I have eaten five hundred cakes, I've eaten my friend the parrot, I've eaten an old woman. What's to keep me from eating an old

man and a donkey?" Slip! Slop! Down went the old man and the donkey.

The cat next met the wedding procession of a king. Behind the king and his new bride marched a column of soldiers and behind them a row of elephants, two by two. The king said to the cat, "Run away, cat, or my elephants might trample you to death."

"Ho!" said the cat. "I've eaten five hundred cakes, I've eaten my friend the parrot, I've eaten an old woman, I've eaten an old man and a donkey. What's to keep me from eating a beggarly king?"

Slip! Slop! Down went the king, the queen, the soldiers, and all the elephants!

The cat went on until he met two land crabs, scuttling along in the dusk. "Run away, cat," they squeaked, "or we will nip you!"

"Ho! Ho! Ho!" laughed the cat, shaking his fat sides. "I've eaten five hundred cakes, I've eaten my friend the parrot, I've eaten an old woman, I've eaten an old man with a donkey, I've eaten a king and a queen, his soldiers, and all his elephants. Shall I run away from land crabs? No. I'll eat you, too!"

Slip! Slop! Down went the land crabs.

When the land crabs got down inside the cat, they found themselves among a crowd of creatures. They could see the unhappy king with his bride, who had fainted. The soldiers were trying to march, and the elephants trumpeted while the donkey brayed as the old man beat it. The old woman and the parrot were there, and last of all, the five hundred cakes neatly piled in a corner.

The land crabs ran around to see what they could do. "Let's nip!" they said. So, nip! nip! nip! they made a round hole in the side of the cat. Nip! nip! nip! until the hole was big enough to let them all walk through. The land crabs scuttled out and away. Then out walked the king, carrying his bride; out walked the soldiers and the elephants, two by two; out walked the old man, driving his donkey; out walked the old woman, giving the cat a piece of her mind; and last of all, out walked the parrot with a cake in each claw!

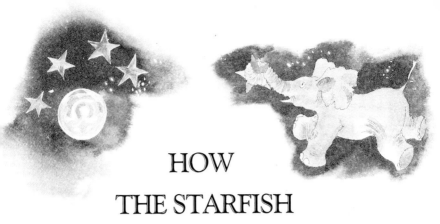

HOW
THE STARFISH
WAS BORN

Donald Bisset

Once upon a time there were seven elephants.

There was a great big elephant and a not-so-big elephant, and an elephant who wasn't quite as large as that, and a middle-sized elephant, and one a bit smaller, and a very small elephant and a tiny little baby elephant.

They were all standing on top of a hill near the seaside watching the stars shine. The night was very dark and the stars twinkled brightly.

The fish in the sea were watching the stars too. And whenever they saw a falling star, they dived under the water to look for it because it seemed to them to have fallen into the sea.

"Let's try and catch a falling star," said the great big elephant.

"Oh yes, let's!" said the others.

So the great big elephant picked up the not-so-big elephant in his trunk, and the not-so-big elephant picked up the elephant who wasn't quite as large as that, and the elephant who wasn't quite as large as that picked up the middle-sized elephant, and the middle-sized elephant picked up the one who was a bit smaller, and the elephant who was a bit smaller picked up the very small elephant, and the very small elephant picked up the tiny little baby elephant.

Then the great big elephant threw all the others out into the sky towards a falling star. And when they had gone some way the not-so-big elephant threw the others farther still. And when *they* had gone some way the elephant who wasn't quite as large as that threw the middle-sized elephant and the other three as far as *he* could. And then the middle-sized elephant threw the one who was a bit smaller and the other two. And then the one who was a bit smaller threw the very small elephant and the baby elephant. And when they had nearly reached the falling star, the very small elephant threw the tiny little baby elephant; and the tiny little baby elephant caught the falling star in his trunk and gave it to the very small elephant, and the very small elephant gave it to the one who was a little larger, and the one who was a little larger gave it to the middle-sized elephant, and the middle-sized elephant gave it to the next biggest elephant, who gave it to the next one, and he gave it to the great big elephant, who gave it to a fish who swallowed it and became a starfish.

THE WITCH AND THE LITTLE VILLAGE BUS

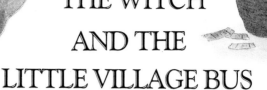

Margaret Stuart Barry

Simon was late for school. So that was how he came to jump on the village bus. And that was how he happened to meet Ginny the witch. He had sat down next to her before he had properly noticed her.

She was a very ugly old witch. She had a pale green face, tiny red eyes like hot cinders, a spot on the end of her long nose, and grey hair which reached down to her knees. Simon was pleased. He liked witches. He hoped she was going to be a really wicked old witch like the ones he had read about.

"What have you got in your bag?" he asked her.

"In my bag? – My magic wand, of course, my Post Office Savings Book, and my knitting."

"Oh," said Simon.

He was a little disappointed. He had hoped that the witch would have had a black toad, or at least a couple of dead spiders. They were passing the school gates, but Simon was too interested to notice.

"Fares please," said the conductor. Simon paid his fare.

"Fares," said the conductor to the witch.

"You forgot to say 'please'," reminded Ginny the witch.

"Why should I say 'please' to an old witch like you," said the conductor, rudely.

"Because it's manners," replied the witch.

"Fares!" snapped the conductor.

"If you do not say 'please', I shall change your silly old bus into something else."

The conductor was now very cross. "Shan't," he said.

At that, the witch opened her handbag and started to search for her wand. As soon as she found it, she changed the bus into a fast express train.

"Wheeeeeee!" went the fast express train. It shot down the village street, through the red lights, and out on to the motorway. On the motorway was a big sign which said – LONDON 50 MILES.

"Hey!" shouted Farmer Spud. "I do not want to go to London. I want to go to Little Hampton to buy a pig."

"Hey!" shouted Mrs Gummidge. "I do not want to go to London either. I want to go to Little Hampton to buy some shoelaces."

"Hey!" said the bus driver. "I do not know how to drive this thing. It is much too fast."

Ginny the witch said nothing. She took her knitting out of her bag and began to knit, very fast. Simon was delighted.

It was not very long before the roaring train reached London. There were cars and buses everywhere. The train was bumping into them one after another.

"This is terrible!" said the conductor. "Stop, stop it!"

"I will if you say 'please'. Otherwise I shall change your silly old train into something else."

"I will not say 'please' to a witch," shouted the rude conductor.

"Suit yourself," said Ginny. She put away her knitting, searched again for her wand, and changed the train into a green caterpillar.

"Help!" cried Farmer Spud, falling off.

"Help!" cried Mrs Gummidge, falling off also.

"Help! Help!" cried the conductor and the bus driver.

The caterpillar was far too slippery to ride on. It was also much too small. The passengers were obliged to walk alongside it.

"This is ridiculous!" complained Farmer Spud. "I have never been on a bus like this in the whole of my life."

"You are not on it man, are you!" snapped Mrs Gummidge, irritably.

"Watch it!" cried the bus driver. "It's going down that grid!"

Laughing, Simon rescued the little caterpillar and set it on its way again. It was actually a great deal of trouble and bother watching the caterpillar. First it went this way, and then the other. It did not seem to have any

clear idea where it wanted to go. The bus driver was
extremely worried about it. He had to get his bus back to
the Depot by six o'clock. It was already half past four.
Suddenly a big policeman stepped into the road to direct
the traffic.

"Watch out!" gasped the bus driver. "You're stepping
on our bus!"

The big London policeman looked around in all
directions. He could not see a bus. He could see only a
bus driver, a conductor, a farmer, an old woman, a small
boy, and a very ugly witch.

"I'm busy," he said. "Mind out."

"This is terrible," moaned the bus driver. "For
goodness sake, say 'please' to the old witch."

"I cannot possibly," said the conductor. "I never say
'please' to witches."

26

"Suit yourself," said Ginny. She had almost finished her knitting.

It was nearing the Rush Hour. The Rush Hour is a terrible thing. Trains and buses and cars and people rush about everywhere in a great hurry. They squash and push and squeeze each other. There is certainly no room for a caravan drawn by six cart-horses. So this is what the witch decided to do. She pulled out her wand and changed the little caterpillar into a handsome caravan, drawn by six cart-horses. The caravan took up a lot more room than the caterpillar had done. Moreover, the cart-horses could not tell green lights from red lights: they clattered clumsily on. They did not understand what the policemen were shouting about. When cars and buses kicked them, they kicked back with a will.

"This is great!" cried Simon. "It's better than school!"

"This is monstrous!" cried the bus driver.

"My pig! My shoelaces!" cried Farmer Spud and Mrs Gummidge together, looking at the time. It was now five o'clock. They would never get back to the Depot. The six cart-horses caught sight of Hyde Park. It looked nice and green. They trotted in for a feed of grass.

"They can't do that!" exclaimed the bus driver. "There isn't time!"

"It's your conductor who is making us late – not my horses," said Ginny. "Anyway, I'm tired." She hung up her hat on a branch and sat down under a tree for a nap.

"She's going to sleep!" cried Farmer Spud, indignantly. He shook her, and said, "Wake up, wake up – you bad old witch."

"Go away," yawned Ginny. "I've had a hard day."

No one knew what to do – except Simon. He had run off to play with the horses. He did not mind one bit how late it was.

Then Mrs Gummidge got very cross. "Now just you listen to me, conductor," she scolded – prodding him in the tummy with her umbrella. "It is high time we went home. We have had enough of this nonsense. Mend your manners and say 'please' to that old witch at once."

"But I never say 'please' to . . ."

Mrs Gummidge poked her umbrella a little harder.

"Oh, very well," grumbled the conductor. He was worn out anyway. He shuffled over to Ginny.

"Fares please," he said in a sulky voice.

Ginny opened one red eye, and said, "Pardon?"

"Fares please," said the conductor again.

Ginny put one finger into her ear and rubbed it very hard until it squeaked. "Pardon?" she said again.

"Fares – please." This time the conductor said it very politely.

"Now that's better!" declared the witch.

She whisked out her wand and she changed the caravan and the six cart-horses into a big jet. Everybody scrambled in as fast as they could.

"Zooooom!" went the jet – and before the bus driver, or the conductor, or the farmer, or the old woman, or the little boy had time to think – they were in Little Hampton.

The shops were shut, so it was too late for Farmer Spud to buy his pig, or Mrs Gummidge her shoelaces. But it was still only one minute before six o'clock – just enough time for the witch to change the big jet plane back into the village bus.

"Thank you, Madam," said the conductor – very politely.

"You're welcome," said the witch. "Any time."

Then she went home with Simon, to explain to Simon's mother why he was home a little late for tea.

29

THE
CROSS
PHOTOGRAPH

Dorothy Edwards

A long time ago, when I was a little girl with a naughty little sister who was younger than myself, our mother made us a beautiful coat each.

They were lovely red coats with black buttons to do them up with and curly-curly black fur on them to keep us warm. We were very proud children when we put our new red coats on.

Our mother was proud too, because she had never made any coats before, and she said, "I know! You shall have your photographs taken. Then we can always remember how smart they look."

So our proud mother took my naughty little sister and me to have our photographs taken in our smart red coats.

The man in the photographer's shop was very smart too. He had curly-curly black hair *just* like the fur on our new coats, and he had a pink flower in his buttonhole and a yellow handkerchief that he waved and waved when he took our photographs.

There were lots of pictures in the shop. There were

pictures of children, and ladies being married, and ladies smiling, and gentlemen smiling, and pussy-cats with long fur, and black-and-white rabbits. All those pictures! And the smart curly-curly man had taken every one himself!

He said we could go and look at his pictures while he talked to our mother, so I went round and looked at them. But do you know, my naughty little sister wouldn't look. She stood still as still and quiet as quiet, and she shut her eyes.

Yes, she did. She shut her eyes and wouldn't look at anything. She was being a stubborn girl, and when the photographer-man said, "Are you both ready?" my bad little sister kept her eyes shut and said, "No."

Our mother said, "But surely you want your photograph taken?"

But my naughty little sister kept her eyes shut tight as tight, and said, "No taken! No taken!" And she got so cross, and shouted so much, that the curly man said, "All right then. I will just take your big sister by herself."

"I will take a nice photograph of your big sister," said the photographer-man, "and she will be able to show it to all her friends. Wouldn't you like a photograph of yourself to show to your friends?"

My naughty little sister did

31

want a photograph of herself to show to her friends, but she would not say so. She just said, "No photograph!"

So our mother said, "Oh well, it looks as if it will be only one picture then, for we can't keep this gentleman waiting all day."

So the photographer-man made me stand on a box-thing. There was a little table on the box-thing, and I had to put my hand on the little table and stand up straight and smile.

There was a beautiful picture of a garden on the wall behind me. It was such a big picture that when the photograph was taken it looked just as if I was standing in a real garden. Wasn't that a clever idea?

When I was standing quite straight and quite smiley, the curly photographer-man shone a lot of bright lights, and then he got his big black camera-on-legs and said, "Watch for the dickey-bird!" And he waved and waved his yellow handkerchief. And then 'click!' said the camera, and my picture was safe inside it.

"That's all," said the man, and he helped me to get down.

Now, what do you think? While the man was taking my picture, my little sister had opened her eyes to peep, and when she saw me standing all straight and smily in my beautiful new coat, and heard the man say, "Watch for the dickey-bird," and saw him wave his yellow handkerchief, she stared and stared.

The man said, "That was all right, wasn't it?" and I said, "Yes, thank you."

Then the curly man looked at my little sister and he

32

saw that her eyes weren't shut any more so he said, "Are you going to change your mind now?"

And what do you think? My little sister changed her mind. She stopped being stubborn. She changed her mind and said, "Yes, please," like a good polite child. You see, she hadn't known anything about photographs before, and she had been frightened, but when she saw me having my picture taken, and had seen how easy it was, she hadn't been frightened any more.

She let the man lift her on to the box-thing. She was so small though, that he took the table away and found a little chair for her to sit on, and gave her a teddy-bear to hold.

Then he said, "Smile nicely now," and my naughty little sister smiled very beautifully indeed.

The man said, "Watch for the dickey-bird," and he waved his yellow handkerchief to her, and 'click', my naughty little sister's photograph had been taken too!

But what do you think? *She hadn't kept smiling.* When the photographs came home for us to look at, there was my little sister holding the teddy-bear and looking as cross as cross.

Our mother *was* surprised. She said, "I thought the man told you to *smile!*"

And what do you think that funny girl said? She said, "I did smile, but there wasn't any dickey-bird, so I stopped."

My mother said, "Oh dear! We shall have to have it taken all over again!"

But our father said, "No, I like this one. It is such a natural picture. I like it as it is." And he laughed and laughed and laughed and laughed.

My little sister liked the cross picture very much too, and sometimes, when she hadn't anything else to do, she climbed up to the looking-glass and made cross faces at herself. *Just* like the cross face in the photograph!

ROUND THE WORLD
WITH A TYRE

Edward Blishen

When I was not quite five, I lived near a dump. This was a long time ago, and there weren't half the cars on the road that there are now. But on the dump, which was where people threw things away, there were always hundreds of tyres.

My friend Harry Carter and I loved that dump. We never knew what we'd find. There'd be marvellous tins and beautiful battered boxes. There'd be broken chairs, and tables with only three legs. And there'd be tyres. Every time we went there, we admired the tins and boxes. We tried to make the three-legged tables stand up, which they wouldn't. Then we'd choose a tyre and bowl it away. The bigger the better. I can't remember Harry's face now. That's because it was usually hidden behind the tyre he was bowling down the street.

Sometimes we'd meet another boy bowling *his* tyre in the opposite direction. And because we were smaller than our tyres, they'd collide and fall over with a great hollow rubbery clunk. And there we'd stand, making angry faces at each other.

"You knocked my tyre over!"

"No, I didn't! *You* knocked *my* tyre over!"

It could lead to battle.

It must have been awkward in those days for any grown-ups who made the mistake of being around. The streets were full of boys bowling enormous tyres! Sometimes, if there was a bit of a slope, we'd lose control. The tyres would roll faster than we could follow them, and if they headed for some unlucky adult, then we'd either have to run after them . . . or just run away.

When the day was over, and I had to go in to bed, I always had the problem of how best to hide my tyre. It had two enemies. One was the boy next door, who wanted it for himself. If I hid it under the hedge at the back of the garden, and my mum called me in at six, and his mum called him in at a quarter past six, he had a quarter of an hour to hunt around and find it. Then he'd take it next door and hide it under *his* hedge, and next morning there'd be another battle.

"That's *my* tyre!"

"Prove it!"

I never could. If I said it was a tyre off a motorbike, he'd say his was a tyre off a motorbike too. If I said mine was an extra-big one with DUNLOP written on it, he'd say his was an extra-big one with DUNLOP written on it.

Then I'd lost my tyre.

Its other enemy was my dad or my mum. *He'd* told me hundreds of times that he didn't want to find dirty old tyres under his back hedge. *She'd* said she was tired of washing the dirt off my hands after I'd spent all day bowling those terrible filthy tyres all over the street. And Mrs Grumbler next door had complained that my tyre had only just missed her.

Dirty tyres? Terrible filthy tyres? What a way to talk about tyres! And Mrs Grumbler ought to have told my mum how *clever* I was to miss her. She ought to have said,

"Your lad knows how to control a tyre. You must be proud of him. I've been watching, and he's the best of the lot."

So sometimes I was happy, because I had this particularly fine tyre and it was safely hidden and I could lie in bed and think about bowling it up and down the street all the next day. And sometimes I was miserable, because my tyre had gone and my mum said I wasn't to go back to the dump and get another one.

"No dump today," she'd say. She'd made me look my best, ready for a visit to Auntie Hilda that afternoon; and look at my face already! "You'd think it had never known what it was to be washed!" I was probably the dirtiest boy there'd ever been in the whole world. "Heaven knows what Auntie Hilda will think!"

But I knew what Auntie Hilda would think. That was because she always said it.

"I give up! Boys are the limit! I think they'd *eat* dirt if you served it up for their dinner!"

If my mum and my aunts had their way, I'd spend my whole life in the bathroom. When one of them was tired of washing me, then another would come and take over.

But I remember one day when all was well. All was wonderfully well!

Harry and I had two of the best tyres we'd ever found on the dump. He had DUNLOP written on his, and on mine I had a pair of wings. It was like an angel without a head. The wings seemed to make this tyre bowl along

faster than any I'd ever had before. It was the greatest tyre ever, and of course it was in the hands of the greatest-ever bowler of tyres!

Harry and I set off at a spanking pace in the direction of Africa.

Well, I thought Africa probably wasn't very far beyond the church

at the bottom of the road. I'd gone past it once or twice
with my dad, but only a step or two. The other way was
the dump, and that was more or less the end of the world
in that direction. To the left there was a road we weren't
allowed to go down. To the right there was a steam
laundry. There were great wheels inside and outside the
building, and immense leather straps ran round the
wheels. The laundry shook with the movement of those
straps. There was a funnel on the roof that puffed out
steam. It was as if the laundry was gasping for breath. It

smelt too, of . . . laundry, and soap, and being clean. Sometimes I'd think that Mum and Auntie Hilda might take me to the laundry and simply leave me there, to be everlastingly scrubbed and hung up to dry and ironed.

So there we were, Harry and I, that good day, setting off towards Africa. That is, as we thought, down the road to the church. Once there, we'd go twice round the war memorial, and then back home. Mission completed.

And that's where the good day became a bad day.

At some point, unable to see over our tyres, we went wrong. Instead of stopping short at Africa, we headed for the North Pole. That's to say, as I know now, we turned towards the laundry. But we didn't reach it. If we had, we'd have heard all that puffing and known where we were. Instead, we must somehow have turned into a side road.

The tyres were moving beautifully. It was one of those afternoons that go on for ever. We'd never been better than this at tyre bowling. It was definitely the best afternoon of our lives.

But after a time I wondered what had happened to the church.

Harry must have wondered that, too. Because suddenly – he was ahead of me – his tyre began to tremble, and then slowly it fell sideways and then lay flat on the pavement. And I stopped bowling too, and *my* tyre trembled and fell flat on the pavement. And now we could see we weren't anywhere near the church. We weren't even in Africa. We weren't at the North Pole. If there was some terrible name for where we were, it must be Australia. I'd heard of Australia, and it was about as far from home as you could get.

Harry said, "Where are we?"

Well, the houses Harry and I lived in were small and all alike. The houses we were looking at now were big and all different. I remember one house had a path leading to a front door that had glass over it. You walked up to the front door under glass! I'd never seen anything like it! Our own houses had simple short paths, and simple front doors. Some of the front doors here had great pillars, and little roofs of their own. All *our* houses were known by numbers. I lived in number 232. These houses had names. There wasn't a number to be seen.

Where were we?

Harry said, "What shall we do?"

Mum had said if I was ever lost I was to say I came from 232 East Barnet Road. But who was I to say this to? There was nobody to be seen.

In *our* streets, there were always kids, and always quite a few grown-ups. In *this* street, there was nobody.

Australia was empty and silent.

I said, "Let's go back the way we came!"

It was the only idea I had. Perhaps, if you'd gone wrong, the thing to do was to turn round and . . . do what you'd done before, but backwards.

So Harry and I turned and picked up our tyres and began bowling back the way we'd come. Except, of course, that we weren't at all sure *which* way we'd come.

I suppose it took ten minutes or so, that return journey. I remember it taking for ever. We just bowled along blindly. This time I was in the lead, and I didn't dare to think of where I was going. I just went. The pavement flew past, grey, grey, grey. All the pavements were the same. Wherever I looked, there was nothing I recognized.

And then . . .

I still remember the joy of it. To think that, after all, I'd see Mum again. And Dad. I'd have my tea, after all. I was even, at that moment, glad to think I'd see Auntie Hilda again.

At that moment, I WAS GLAD!

Because, to my left, I heard a puffing. I heard the flapping sound the great belts made. I smelt the smell of great cleanliness. I knew where we were.

We'd found the laundry . . .

It wasn't long after that when I went to school for the first time and Miss Stout, our teacher, told us about the world. The world was very big, she said. It was very much bigger than East Barnet. And it was round. There was a man called Christopher Columbus who'd bowled his tyre . . . no, he'd sailed his ship across the huge sea, believing the world was round and he was safe. Lots of people at the time thought that Christopher Columbus would sail off the edge of it and go spinning to his death in space.

But they were wrong, and Christopher Columbus was right. He proved the world was round.

I thought, and I said to Harry, that Christopher Columbus might have been the first to prove it, but Harry and I hadn't been far behind. That afternoon when we couldn't find the church, we'd proved the world was round.

Well, obviously, Harry and I had been round it.

THE DONKEY THAT HELPED FATHER CHRISTMAS

Elizabeth Clark

It was Christmas Eve and the night was very quiet and still. The stars and the little moon sparkled in the sky and the hoar-frost sparkled on the grass. It was a bright clear night, but it was very cold.

The old Donkey who lived on the common was limping along towards a great clump of tall ragged furze-bushes. He knew of a sheltered place in the middle of the clump – almost like a little cave. It would be warmer there, and he might find a tuft of grass, that was not frosted, to eat when morning came.

He was a rough-coated, shaggy old Donkey who had been left behind by some gypsies who had camped on the common in the spring, because he was too lame to pull their little cart. He had lived there ever since. He was still rather lame, but he limped about slowly and comfortably and munched grass and green leaves. He was glad there was no heavy load to pull along hard roads and rough lanes and nobody to beat his poor little back with a thick stick. Nobody was unkind to him. In fact, nobody noticed him; he was just a shaggy, shabby old Donkey.

Sometimes he would have liked a little more company. Donkeys are friendly creatures, and he missed the old white horse that drew the gypsies' van and the little brown dog that barked so loudly and the little black cat that sat on the steps of the van blinking and purring when the sun shone. He even missed the children, though they had teased him and bothered him by climbing on his tired old back to ride.

That Christmas Eve the Donkey was feeling very lonely. The brown cow that lived on the common had been driven into her shed because the weather had turned so cold. She was glad to go, and the Donkey had heard the old woman who came to fetch her say, "Come along, Brownie; come along, my dear, into your nice warm shed. There's some warm straw and some beautiful hay and a feed of chopped swedes for a treat, because tomorrow is Christmas Day." (Swedes are like very big turnips and cows like them very much.)

The Donkey had heard of Christmas. He did not know much about it, but if it was anything to do with hay and turnips he was sure it must be comfortable. He had once tasted a turnip-top and now and again he had a mouthful of hay that had been stolen from somebody's stack.

"Hay and chopped swedes," he said to himself, "hay and chopped swedes." The thought made him feel hungry, and he put his nose down and snuffled and blew among the grass tufts and tried to find something to eat. But the grass was all stiff and frosted. It tickled his nose and made him sneeze and sneeze.

"Broo-oo-oof," said the Donkey (which is as near as I can get to writing down a donkey's sneeze for you). He shook his head hard till his ears flapped, and brayed a long mournful bray.

"Eee-aw-ee-aw-ee-aw-ee-aw-aw-aw-*aw*," said the Donkey. He ended with a kind of choky snort and stood there with his neck stretched out and his ears laid back and his tail tucked in between his legs – a sad, shaggy, grumpy old Donkey.

Down in the valley where the village stood the church clock began to strike just as he finished braying. It struck twelve; each stroke sounded loud and clear in the stillness. And as it finished striking there came another sound. You and I might never have heard it, it was so tiny and soft. But animals can hear a great many more things than most people – and can see them too. The Donkey pricked up his ears and stood listening.

There was a little shivery, silvery tinkling in the air, a pretty, tiny, far-off sound as if the stars above were

46

tingling. It came nearer and nearer still. Then it seemed to the Donkey that somewhere overhead something went rushing by with a clear sweet ringing like silver bells and a noise of far-away hoofs galloping fast.

It was an exciting kind of noise. It made the Donkey feel as if he must gallop too. He could not remember galloping since he was a baby donkey with his mother; all his life had been spent jog-trotting with a cart. But he tucked in his head and his ears and his tail as donkeys do when they gallop, and he was just going to try – in spite of his game leg – when he heard another sound. Somebody was coming up the hill.

The Donkey waited and listened. He could hear footsteps crunching a little on the frosty grass. Presently he could see somebody coming towards him – somebody

tall and big in a long shaggy white fur coat with a warm white fur hood pulled over his head and big fur-topped boots upon his feet. As he came nearer, the Donkey could see that he had a long white beard and under his white fur hood his eyes shone and twinkled like two bright stars. There was a big sack upon his shoulders. It was tied in the middle, but both ends bulged and hung down as if it was full of queerly shaped things.

He came and stood by the Donkey. He was puffing a little as if the sack was heavy to carry up the hill. His breath was like a little cloud in the frosty air. He looked at the Donkey and the Donkey looked at him.

The Donkey was feeling still more excited; he was happy too, not grumpy any more. There seemed to be a wonderful, kind, warm, friendly feeling all around. He was remembering something the brown cow had told him about Christmas Eve and he was longing to ask a question. But he thought it would be more polite to wait till he was spoken to, so he stayed still and quiet. And then a very kind voice said, "Happy Christmas, friend Donkey. I heard you calling and you sounded lonely, so I came."

"I *was* lonely," said the Donkey, "and I'm glad you came. Excuse my asking, but would you mind telling me who you are?"

And the friendly voice said, "Some people call me Father Christmas and some say Santa Klaus. It's all the same really. They both stand for loving-kindness."

"I remember now," said the Donkey; "the brown cow told me about you. But *she* said," said the Donkey in a puzzled voice, "that you came in a sledge with reindeer."

"So I do," said Father Christmas. "So I do. But I've sent them home tonight. It's after twelve o'clock. Didn't you hear the sledge-bells go by?"

"Oh-h-h!" said the Donkey, "so *that* was it."

"Yes," said Father Christmas, "that was it. They've been a long, long way tonight. Here, there, and everywhere we've been, all over the country – north, south, east and west – finding the children. Children from Birmingham, children from Bristol, children from London, and children from Plymouth, children from Newcastle and Liverpool and Hull and ever so many other places. Out of the towns they've gone and into the country. All over the place they are this Christmas, and wherever they are we've found them."

"So when twelve o'clock struck," said Father Christmas, "'Home!' I said to the reindeer. I tied up the reins and let them go, and off they went to their stable. There's only this sackful now to take to Green Lane Hollow and a few places on the way. I can carry that myself."

The Donkey looked at the sack. It was large and it was bulgy and certainly it was heavy.

"Green Lane Hollow is twelve miles away," he said. He knew all the lanes and hills and hollows. He had pulled his little cart all round the country with the gypsies.

Father Christmas smiled at him. "If I keep on walking," he said, "I shall get there."

"Couldn't I help?" said the Donkey. "I could carry the sack."

"Why," said Father Christmas, "so you could." He looked at the Donkey very affectionately. "But what about your leg?"

"I can manage," said the Donkey stoutly.

"So you shall," said Father Christmas. "So you shall."

He laid the sack across the Donkey's back and they set out. Across the common they went and down a narrow lane; up a steep hill and along the high-road. On and on they went. The sack was heavy, but the Donkey's back was strong, and though his leg was stiff it was wonderful how little it hurt.

On and on they went. Sometimes the road dipped into hollows where it was dark; then Father Christmas went

ahead, to show the way. There was a kind of shining round about him and it was quite easy to follow him.

But he mostly walked beside the Donkey with his hand resting on the Donkey's shoulders, just where the dark cross-mark showed on the shaggy mouse-coloured coat. It gave the Donkey a wonderful happy kind of warm glow to feel it there.

Every now and again they stopped to leave a packet or a bundle by the door of a house or cottage. The Donkey could feel that the sack was growing lighter. But there was still a good deal left in it when they came to the top of the long lane that led down to Green Lane Hollow.

Father Christmas looked up at the sky and nodded. "It's not long now till daylight," he said.

It certainly was a long lane. The stars were beginning to look pale and silvery and there was a pinky look in the sky before they came to the bottom of the hill and saw a long white cottage with a thatched roof. It looked like a little farm. There were comfortable little noises of hens clucking and waking and a cow lowing in a shed.

The house looked fast asleep. All the windows were dark and all the curtains were drawn. But as the Donkey and Father Christmas came down the road they saw a little chink of light in a window and smoke began to fluff out of a chimney.

"That's old Mrs Honeywell," said Father Christmas. "She's stirring up the fire. The house will be wide awake in a moment. It's time for me to be going."

They went quietly along, walking on the grass at the edge of the lane. As they came to the door they could hear Mrs Honeywell trotting about, clattering cups and saucers and clacketing to and fro over the brick floor.

"Happy Christmas," said Father Christmas softly to the Donkey. He stooped and kissed him on his velvety nose. His beard was warm and tickly and soft. The Donkey wanted to sneeze – but the sneeze turned into a bray – a most tremendous bray.

"Ee-aw-ee-aw-ee-aw," said the Donkey. He heard someone give a little chuckle and he felt something touch his ears. He looked about, but Father Christmas was gone.

But the cottage was awake – wide awake. The door flew open and there stood old Mrs Honeywell. The curtains rustled back and the windows creaked up and

there was Master Honeywell leaning out of one window and two small boys at the next window and two more at the window beyond. They were all staring at the Donkey. And who wouldn't stare if they looked out of their window on Christmas Day in the morning and saw a Donkey standing there, with a sack upon his back?

"Bless me!" said Mrs Honeywell. "Where did *that* come from? Bless me!" she said again, "it's got a ticket on its head!"

She came close to the Donkey and looked. Father Christmas had left a message. Hanging to the Donkey's ears was a neat little label. It said, 'I bring Happy Christmas to Green Lane Hollow.'

"Well, I never *did!*" said Mrs Honeywell. "Come along down, Father – come along, Dick and Tommy and Charlie and John."

The four boys came tumbling downstairs with Master Honeywell behind them. They had had lots of surprises since they came out of London to live with Master and Mrs Honeywell – but this was the biggest surprise of all.

Mrs Honeywell patted the Donkey and gave him an apple to eat. Then she turned the sack out on the kitchen floor.

There was a football and four red jerseys for the boys. There was a warm blue woollen coat for Mrs Honeywell and a knitted waistcoat for Master Honeywell. There was a plum-pudding in a basin and a bottle of sweets. No wonder the sack had felt *bumpy!*

But the boys seemed to think the Donkey was the best present of all. They patted him and petted him. Mrs Honeywell gave him another apple and Master Honeywell gave him an armful of hay. Everyone was happy and kind, and I believe the Donkey was happiest of all.

That was Christmas Day, and he has been there ever since. He has grown quite sleek; the boys have brushed and curry-combed his coat. Master Honeywell has doctored his lame leg, and sometimes he pulls a little cart that is never too heavily loaded and trots along the road to the village when Mrs Honeywell goes shopping.

He helps with the hay-harvest in the summer, and when the boys are not in school, one or other of them is generally on his back. He is a happy and contented old Donkey.

THE OLD WOMAN
AND
HER PIG

An English tale

An old woman was sweeping her house, and she found a little crooked sixpence. "What," said she, "shall I do with this little sixpence? I will go to market, and buy a little pig."

As she was coming home, she came to a stile: but the piggy wouldn't go over the stile.

She went a little farther, and she met a dog. So she said to him, "Dog! dog! bite pig; piggy won't go over the stile; and I shan't get home tonight." But the dog wouldn't.

She went a little farther, and she met a stick. So she said, "Stick! stick! beat dog! dog won't bite pig; piggy won't get over the stile; and I shan't get home tonight." But the stick wouldn't.

She went a little farther, and she met a fire. So she said, "Fire! fire! burn stick; stick won't beat dog; dog won't bite pig; piggy won't get over the stile; and I shan't .get home tonight." But the fire wouldn't.

56

She went a little farther, and she met some water. So she said, "Water! water! quench fire; fire won't burn stick; stick won't beat dog; dog won't bite pig; piggy won't get over the stile; and I shan't get home tonight." But the water wouldn't.

She went a little farther, and she met an ox. So she said, "Ox! ox! drink water; water won't quench fire; fire won't burn stick; stick won't beat dog; dog won't bite pig; piggy won't get over the stile; and I shan't get home tonight." But the ox wouldn't.

She went a little farther, and she met a butcher. So she said, "Butcher! butcher! kill ox; ox won't drink water; water won't quench fire; fire won't burn stick; stick won't beat dog; dog won't bite pig; piggy won't get over the stile; and I shan't get home tonight." But the butcher wouldn't.

She went a little farther, and she met a rope. So she said, "Rope! rope! hang butcher; butcher won't kill ox; ox won't drink water; water won't quench fire; fire won't

burn stick; stick won't beat dog; dog won't bite pig; piggy won't get over the stile; and I shan't get home tonight." But the rope wouldn't.

She went a little farther, and she met a rat. So she said, "Rat! rat! gnaw rope; rope won't hang butcher; butcher won't kill ox; ox won't drink water; water won't quench fire; fire won't burn stick; stick won't beat dog; dog won't bite pig; piggy won't get over the stile; and I shan't get home tonight." But the rat wouldn't.

She went a little farther, and she met a cat. So she said, "Cat! cat! kill rat; rat won't gnaw rope; rope won't hang butcher; butcher won't kill ox; ox won't drink water; water won't quench fire;

fire won't burn stick; stick won't beat dog; dog won't bite pig; piggy won't get over the stile; and I shan't get home tonight." But the cat said to her, "If you will go to yonder cow, and fetch me a saucer of milk, I will kill the rat." So away went the old woman to the cow.

But the cow said to her, "If you will go to yonder hay-stack, and fetch me a handful of hay, I'll give you the milk." So away went the old woman to the hay-stack; and she brought the hay to the cow.

As soon as the cow had eaten the hay, she gave the old woman the milk; and away she went with it in a saucer to the cat.

As soon as the cat had lapped up the milk, the cat began to kill the rat; the rat began to gnaw the rope; the rope began to hang the butcher; the butcher began to kill the ox; the ox began to drink the water; the water began to quench the fire; the fire began to burn the stick; the stick began to beat the dog; the dog began to bite the pig; the little pig in a fright jumped over the stile; and so the old woman got home that night.

THE GIANT
WHO THREW
TANTRUMS

David L Harrison

At the foot of Thistle Mountain lay a village.
In the village lived a little boy who liked to go walking. One Saturday afternoon he was walking in the woods when he was startled by a terrible noise.

He scrambled quickly behind a bush.

Before long a huge giant came stamping down the path.

He looked upset.

"Tanglebangled ringlepox!" the giant bellowed. He banged his head against a tree until the leaves shook off like snowflakes. "Franglewhangled whippersnack!" the giant roared. Yanking up the tree, he whirled it around his head and knocked down twenty-seven other trees.

Muttering to himself, he stalked up the path towards the top of Thistle Mountain.

The little boy hurried home.

"I just saw a giant throwing a tantrum!" he told everyone in the village.

They only smiled.

"There's no such thing as a giant," the mayor assured him.

"He knocked down twenty-seven trees," said the little boy.

"Must have been a tornado," the weatherman said with a nod. "Happens around here all the time."

The next Saturday afternoon the little boy again went walking. Before long he heard a horrible noise. Quick as lightning, he slipped behind a tree.

Soon the same giant came storming down the path. He still looked upset.

"Pollywogging frizzelsnatch!" he yelled. Throwing himself down, he pounded the ground with both fists.

Boulders bounced like hailstones.

Scowling, the giant puckered his lips into an 'O'.

He drew in his breath sharply. It sounded like somebody slurping soup.

"Pooh!" he cried.

Grabbing his left foot with both hands, the giant hopped on his right foot up the path towards the top of Thistle Mountain.

The little boy hurried home.

"That giant's at it again," he told everyone. "He threw such a tantrum that the ground trembled!"

"Must have been an earthquake," the police chief said. "Happens around here sometimes."

The next Saturday afternoon the little boy again went walking. Before long he heard a frightening noise.

He dropped down behind a rock.

Soon the giant came fuming down the path. When he reached the little boy's rock, he puckered his lips into an 'O'. He drew in his breath sharply with a loud, rushing-wind sound. "Phooey!" he cried. "I *never* get it right!"

The giant held his breath until his face turned blue and

his eyes rolled up. "Fozzlehumper backawacket!" he panted. Then he lumbered up the path towards the top of Thistle Mountain.

The little boy followed him. Up and up and up he climbed to the very top of Thistle Mountain.

There he discovered a huge cave. A surprising sound was coming from it. The giant was crying!

"All I want is to whistle," he sighed through his tears. "But every time I try, it comes out wrong!"

The little boy had just learned to whistle. He knew how hard it could be. He stepped inside the cave.

The giant looked surprised. "How did *you* get here?"

"I know what you're doing wrong," the little boy said.

When the giant heard that, he leaned down and put his hands on his knees.

"Tell me at once!" he begged.

"You have to stop throwing tantrums," the little boy told him.

"I promise!" said the giant, who didn't want anyone to think he had poor manners.

"Pucker your lips . . ." the little boy said.

"I always do!" the giant assured him.

"Then blow," the little boy added.

"Blow?"

"Blow."

The giant looked as if he didn't believe it. He puckered his lips into an 'O'. He blew. Out came a long, low whistle. It sounded like a railway engine. The giant smiled.

He shouted, "I whistled! Did you hear that? I whistled!"

Taking the little boy's hand, he danced in a circle.

"You're a good friend," the giant said.

"Thank you," said the little boy. "Perhaps some time we can whistle together. But just now I have to go. It's my suppertime."

The giant stood before his cave and waved goodbye.

The little boy seldom saw the giant after that. But the giant kept his promise about not throwing tantrums.

"We never have earthquakes," the mayor liked to say.

"Haven't had a tornado in ages," the weatherman would add.

Now and then they heard a long, low whistle somewhere in the distance.

"Must be a train," the police chief would say.

But the little boy knew his friend the giant was walking up the path towards the top of Thistle Mountain – whistling.

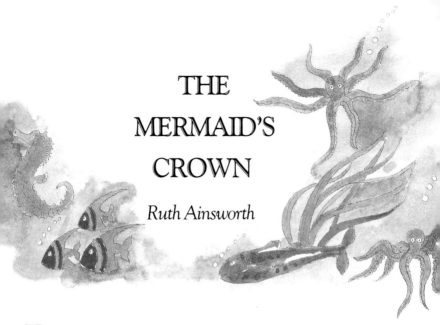

THE
MERMAID'S
CROWN

Ruth Ainsworth

Peter and Rose lived in a cottage by the sea. It had a tiny garden, but that did not matter. There were no parks or playgrounds nearby, but that was not important either. The children always played on the beach, summer and winter.

In the summer they scrambled over the rocks and paddled in the pools, and Rose made houses of stones and sand, with gardens of seaweed and shells. They were pretty enough to live in.

In the winter they often played in wellingtons and sometimes had to shelter in a cave or against a rock. But the beach was lovely to play on, all the year round.

They liked to play on a flat rock, jutting out into the sea with a pool on one side.

One winter's day, Rose was fishing bits of seaweed out of the pool to make a garden. The seaweed was cold and slippery and her hands were frozen, but she had nearly enough when, reaching out for a wavy purple ribbon, she saw something floating deep down.

"Peter, come and help. I can see something lovely but I can't reach it. Hold my legs."

Peter held her legs tightly and she rolled up her sleeve and reached into the icy water.

"I've got it – no, it has slipped away – now I've got it again. Hold tight!"

She brought up something neither child had ever seen before. It was a circle of seaweed, not floppy, but firm, and mixed with the weed were shells and shining stones.

"It's like a crown," said Peter.

"And it's mine," said Rose, putting it on her head. "It's my very own." It fitted perfectly.

Their parents examined it and talked about it, but could not decide how it had got into the pool. Perhaps from a wreck? They thought the pink stones were coral and the yellow ones amber. After a few days of talking and wondering they lost interest.

Rose had only one safe place in the house, a wooden box with a lock which she called her treasure box. She kept the crown in this when she wasn't wearing it.

Christmas was getting near and their father put the

tree in its tub in the sitting-room. That afternoon the children began to decorate it. All the decorations from previous years were kept in a big cardboard box. While they were busy, Rose suddenly cried out:

"Peter! Someone looked in at the window."

Peter turned round, but there was no one there. Then Rose called out again, "Look! Quickly!" This time Peter saw a face for an instant. Then it disappeared. He opened the window and jumped out and a little later appeared at the door, leading someone by the hand. It was a mermaid, or rather a mermaid child, about the size of Rose.

The mermaid had long, golden hair, sad grey eyes, a pale face and a fishy tail. At first she looked round the

room in silence. Then she turned to Rose and spoke.

"I want my crown back."

"So it was yours," said Rose. "I didn't know whose it was. I found it floating in the pool. No one was bothering about it. It's mine now."

"But I want it."

"So do I," said Rose. "Will you have something off the Christmas tree instead? Something pretty?"

The mermaid liked the tree. She touched the baubles and the candles very gently and stroked the glass bird. She looked up at the angel who stood at the very top. Then she pointed to a string of tinsel, shining among the dark pine needles.

"Please. For my head."

Rose untwined the tinsel and put it round the mermaid's hair.

"Look in the glass," she said.

The mermaid balanced on a stool and looked at herself in the mirror on the wall.

"It will do," she said gravely and then, quick as a fish leaping, she flashed across the floor, out of the window, and away.

"I shan't tell mother about the mermaid," said Rose.

They almost forgot about the mermaid as the weeks went by and they saw no sign of her. Rose thought of her when she wore her crown and when she locked it in her treasure box. At Easter time they got their Easter eggs ready. The village shop only had plain chocolate ones but they wrapped them in coloured paper and tied them up with ribbon that their mother had given them. Suddenly they felt they were being watched. There, outside the window, was the mermaid. Peter let her in.

"I want my crown," she said. "The silver one came to pieces, bit by bit. There's nothing left."

"But I want it too," said Rose, "and it's mine now. Will you choose a ribbon instead?"

The mermaid looked at the ribbons and touched a red one.

"For my hair, please."

Peter tied the bow as his bows were better than Rose's. Again the mermaid looked at herself in the mirror. Then, quick as a fish leaping, she slipped across the floor and out of the window and away.

Rose hoped she would never come back again, and once more she did not tell her mother what had happened. She did not often wear the crown either, though she looked at it almost every day. The seaweed still shone as if it were wet.

But it was not many weeks before the mermaid appeared a third time. The children were picking kingcups in the stream when she rose, suddenly, from the reeds nearby.

"I want my crown," she said. "The red one kept slipping off and the fishes nibbled it. It isn't pretty any more."

"You should never have let the old one go if you loved it so much," said Rose. "Shall I make you a wreath of kingcups? A golden crown?"

"A golden crown," repeated the mermaid. "Yes," and she almost smiled.

Rose made the crown like a daisy chain, slitting a stalk with her fingernail and drawing the next flower through. The mermaid looked at herself in the clear water.

"Gold," she whispered. "Better than silver or scarlet."

She flashed through the reeds and grasses and disappeared towards the seashore.

In less than a week she was back, her pale face pressed against the window.

"I must have my crown. The gold one drooped and faded and died. My father is a Lord of the Sea and he is going to a banquet with the other Lords. My mother and I are going too. We must all wear our crowns. So I need mine."

Rose saw two tears on the mermaid's cheeks and this time she did not hesitate.

"You shall have it. I'll fetch it."

She ran upstairs, unlocked her treasure box, and brought the crown down. The mermaid put it on and clapped her hands with joy.

"Come to the flat rock in three days' time," she said, before she flashed through the window. With a twist and a twirl, she was gone.

After three days the children went to the flat rock and there, on a bed of seaweed, was an oyster shell. It was tightly closed. When their father opened it, there was a pearl inside. Rose kept it in her treasure box to be made into a ring for her, when she was older and her fingers had stopped growing.

"That will remind you of the mermaid for ever," said her mother, who now knew the whole story.

"I'll remember her even without a pearl," said Rose. "I'll remember her golden hair and her pale face and her fishy tail, and her lovely crown. I knew it was really hers, not mine."

MOTHER KANGAROO

John Kershaw

A lion, a kangaroo and a monkey lived side by side in a zoo. The lion had a cage, and the monkey had a cage, and the kangaroo had a little hut on a piece of grass between them.

One day, the kangaroo was standing outside the hut, thinking. The lion was cleaning his paws, lying down in a corner of his cage. The monkey was holding on to his bars with one hand, and peeling a banana with the other.

"Fancy being a kangaroo," said the lion. "I can lie down and clean my paws and shake my mane. What can you do?"

The kangaroo said nothing.

"Fancy being a kangaroo," said the monkey. "I can chatter and peel bananas and climb trees. What can *you* do?"

Still the kangaroo said nothing.

"I can yawn and flick my tail," continued the lion.

"You just stand there. Quite still."

The kangaroo didn't say a word.

"I can roll over and tumble about and hang upside-down," said the monkey. "You just stand there. Quite still."

The kangaroo stood there, quite still, and said nothing at all.

"I am very big and strong," said the lion. "You are not."

The kangaroo was silent.

"I am clever," said the monkey. "You are not."

Still the kangaroo said nothing.

Then the lion began to get cross. So did the monkey. But the kangaroo did not.

"I am fierce," said the lion. "I frighten people. You can't even growl."

The kangaroo smiled.

"You can't even rub your eyes," said the monkey, rubbing its eyes.

Suddenly the kangaroo hopped, in one hop, from her hut to the lion's cage, and stared at the lion. Then she turned and hopped, in two hops, from the lion's cage to the monkey's cage. And she stared at the monkey. Then she hopped back to the middle of her piece of grass.

The lion and the monkey both began to laugh.

"Is that all you can do?" they said. "Anyone can hop."

Just then a little voice spoke.

"Not everyone can give her baby a ride in her pocket at the same time," it said. "A mother lion can't and a mother monkey can't."

The lion and the monkey stared in surprise. Sure enough, a little face was peeping over the top of a pocket on the front of Mrs Kangaroo's tummy. The face belonged to a baby kangaroo. The baby hopped out of the pocket and grinned at the lion.

"So there!" he said. Then he grinned at the monkey, and hopped away, into the kangaroo's hut.

Mother Kangaroo smiled at the lion and the monkey.

"Good morning," she said. Then she hopped away too. And the monkey and the lion were quiet for the rest of the day.

THE TOYMAKER'S SHOP

Marie Smith

The shop with the bright yellow door and shiny doorknob was tucked away at the end of a very small street, next to a sweet shop. It had a swinging sign that said THE TOYMAKER'S SHOP.

The Toymaker had lived there for many years. He was famous for making the most beautiful toys. But he broke his glasses; and because he could barely see without them, there was now something wrong with all the toys he made. None of the boys and girls who came into his shop bought anything. Soon they stopped coming altogether, and the bright yellow door remained closed.

Well, for example, the Toymaker had painted the dolls' faces a powdery blue. He had made a grandfather clock that went tock, tock, tock, but never tick, and soldiers that marched around the room backwards. There was a rag doll wearing only one pink shoe, and a dancing doll with no shoes at all. Sinbad the Sailor had two wooden legs, instead of only one. As for the King and Queen puppets, they didn't look like a King and Queen

77

at all except for their crowns made from yellow glass beads. Humpty Dumpty was an egg, all right, but he had a long hairy tail. Clancy the Clown looked too cross to be a clown, and he was sitting in long skinny Jack's box. So Jack-in-the-box was Jack-out-of-the-box, and had to sit on a window-sill.

But the worst mistake of all had been made with Merlin the Wizard. He should have had a wand in his hand, but instead he was carrying a china-blue egg. What's more, his starry hat kept slipping over his eyes.

One night the King decided he could bear it no longer. The little yellow door hadn't opened for weeks. So he called the toys together, cleared his royal throat and said:

"Something really *must* be done! We simply can't go on looking like this!" He looked down at his gown. It should have been purple and splendid, but instead was ragged and grey.

"Do you remember," said the King, "the

silver fairy the Toymaker made before he broke his glasses? He made a wand for her. Someone bought her, but when the Toymaker wrapped her up, she dropped her wand. And he couldn't find it. Do you remember?"

The toys nodded and the King continued.

"It must be here somewhere. Now, if we could find it, the Wizard might be able to do magic with it and make us look as we ought to look."

At once they all began to hunt for the wand. They looked in boxes, big and small. They looked under the stairs. They lifted up the rugs and looked under them. They looked in a tiny yellow teapot that the Toymaker had made with two spouts and no handle. They looked in a big brown jug that had two handles and no spout.

They looked everywhere, but the wand was nowhere to be seen.

The King gave a huge royal sigh.

"If we don't want to stay as we

79

are for ever, we must go on looking," he said. And he took out his royal handkerchief (which the Toymaker had made far too small), mopped his royal brow and sat down next to Sinbad the Sailor.

Now, Sinbad was fast asleep, and he hadn't actually done any looking. To make himself comfortable he'd unscrewed one of his hollow wooden legs and given it to a blue-faced doll to hold for him. Then he'd begun to snore.

That made the King angry, and he tried to take the leg from the doll. Let Sinbad put it on and go looking for the wand like everyone else! But the doll, who was rather afraid of Sinbad, held on to it. And as she struggled with the King, the leg broke in half.

And out of it fell a long, slender stick.

"*There* it is!" cried the King. "It's the wand! It was inside Sinbad's leg!"

The wand shone and glowed, and the King picked it up and gave it to Merlin. The Wizard dropped the china-blue egg, pushed up his hat so he could see what he was doing, stroked his long white beard and touched the King on the head with the wand.

There was a loud bang and a cloud of smoke. And when the smoke had cleared away, every toy had turned into a wooden clothes-peg.

"Great Scott!" cried the Wizard. "What *have* I done?" He looked unhappily at the King who, like the rest, was now a plain dull wooden peg. "I must try again!"

Another explosion. More smoke. And now the toys had become green, hairy *hats*.

In despair Merlin stroked his long white beard twice before waving the wand again. By chance the tip of the wand touched one of the stars on his hat.

There was an enormous bang and another great cloud of smoke. And this time, those awful green hairy hats had turned back into toys. Yet how different they looked! They had become as beautiful and well-made as they should have been.

The King, wearing robes of purple and a golden crown, said to the Wizard,

"Now you know how to use the wand, we must mend the Toymaker's glasses. *At once!*"

They crept up the stairs to the Toymaker's bedroom. His old broken glasses lay on a table beside the bed. The Wizard touched them with his wand, and they became bright and new. Then they crept downstairs again and looked at one another with great satisfaction.

For Sinbad the Sailor now had only one wooden leg. The Wizard's hat stayed on his head. The rag doll and the dancing doll had new shoes. The toy soldiers marched smartly round the room forwards. The dolls' faces had turned pink; and as for the Clown, he had the sort of face a clown ought to have, round and laughing. Long skinny Jack was back in the box where he belonged, and Humpty Dumpty had lost his tail.

As for the grandfather clock going tock, tock, tock for so long, it was now going tick, tock, tick, tock, tick, tock . . .

And the little yellow door was preparing itself for the next day. It knew that when the children looked through the window and saw how beautiful the toys were, they'd be turning the shiny doorknob and pouring into the Toymaker's shop.

A LITTLE BIT
OF COLOUR

Nancy Blishen

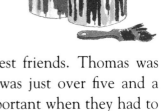

Thomas and Daniel were best friends. Thomas was just over five and Daniel was just over five and a half. Daniel's extra half was important when they had to decide who would choose what games to play, or who would sit next to the driver on the school bus.

"I'm half a year older than you, so *I* can choose," Daniel would say.

Their parents were best friends, too; and that is why the two families lived together in a big, old house. Thomas and his family lived in the flat upstairs, and Daniel and his parents lived downstairs. The boys thought the best thing about the house was that it had a cellar where they played when the weather was bad, and where they could make as much mess as they liked and not get into trouble. There was also a big garden with an orchard full of apple and pear and plum trees, a stable and an old, rather broken-down greenhouse.

It was the last week of the summer holidays. Thomas and Daniel had been to the seaside for two weeks. They had made a den in the cellar, and a camp in the orchard. They had played pirates, and cowboys and Red Indians, crusaders, and explorers. They'd done all the things children love to do in the holidays. Now it was almost time for school to begin again, and they had to think quite hard to find things to do to keep themselves happy.

Then one sunny morning, Daniel woke up and a wonderful idea popped into his head. He couldn't wait to finish his breakfast so he could go and tell Thomas about it. They ran down into the garden and Daniel said,

"Tom, why don't we paint the greenhouse? Not white like it is now, but all the colours of the rainbow!"

"But what would our mums and dads say?" said Thomas, looking worried.

"Oh, that's all right," said Daniel. "I heard my dad say . . ." And he whispered in Thomas's ear.

"GREAT!" said Thomas, and they went into the cellar to collect paint and brushes. On a shelf they found a row of half-empty paint tins – blue, green, orange, yellow and red. They carried these down to the greenhouse and started work.

"Let's paint the doors orange and the window frames blue with yellow edges," said Thomas.

"My favourite colour's red," said Daniel, "so I'm going to have red windows with green edges."

They were so happy and excited that they didn't notice that not all the paint was finishing up on the greenhouse. But then Thomas caught sight of himself in a window pane.

"Hey, Dan, look! I'm the Terrible Monster with Orange Hair!"

Then Daniel peered at himself in the glass. His face was covered with paint spots.

"I'm the Green-Spotted Monster!" he giggled.

Suddenly a window in the upstairs flat opened and Thomas's mother called out.

"Boys, would you like orange juice and a chocolate biscuit? We're coming out . . ."

"Yes, *please!*" they shouted together.

"Do you think they'll like the new greenhouse?" whispered Daniel.

"Of course they will," said Thomas. "It looks *much*

better!" And they stood back and admired the effect of all their hard work.

At that moment they heard steps coming down the path. But suddenly the footsteps stopped. Daniel's mother let out a scream and nearly dropped the tray she was carrying.

"Danny, what on earth have you been doing? Look at your *face* . . . and your *jeans* . . . and the GREENHOUSE! What will Daddy say?"

Thomas's mother was coming down the path behind her.

"I *thought* they were very quiet," she said.

"It's all right," said Daniel. "Daddy will be pleased. I know he will. I heard him say last week, 'What this garden needs is a bit of *colour*!'"

"But he didn't mean PAINT – he meant FLOWERS!" said Daniel's mother. But she didn't sound *quite* so cross.

"Oh," said Thomas and Daniel, looking at each other. Then they looked at their mothers. Their shoulders seemed to be shaking, and funny bubbly noises were coming from inside them. Suddenly they were all laughing helplessly – both mothers *and* Thomas *and* Daniel.

Thomas's mother was the first to recover.

"OK, boys," she said. "We'll forgive you this time. But don't ever do anything like that again without asking first. And now let's get the paint off your hands and we can have tea."

After a lot of scrubbing, which hurt a bit, the two boys were back in the orchard with their drinks and biscuits.

"Dad is funny," said Daniel. "How was I to know that he meant flowers?"

"Well," said Thomas, "what do you think *my* dad said yesterday? I heard him talking to Mr Black next door, and he said, 'We're lucky to be living here and not in a box in a row of other little boxes.' Now, what do you think he meant by *that*?"

"I dunno," said Daniel. "But it might have been fun to live in a box. Don't you think so, Tom?"

"Except when it rained," said Thomas.

And the idea made them laugh so much that they forgot they didn't quite know what their dads would say when they came home that evening and discovered the Rainbow Greenhouse.

THE KING WHO WANTED TO WALK ON THE MOON

There was once a king who wanted nothing so much as to walk on the moon. When he ought to have been ruling his country he was sitting about, thinking of the moon. There it was, up above his head. He could see it. Some nights, when it was bright and full, he felt he could touch it. But it was out of reach.

Being a king, he was used to doing anything he wished. But wish as much as he would, this was something he could *not* do. The king could not walk on the moon.

But one day he had an idea. Of course, of course! Build a tower! He would call together all the carpenters in his kingdom and order them to build a tower. Then he would climb it and step from the top straight on to the moon. That was it!

But the carpenters made long faces.

"Build a tower to the sky?" they cried.

"Yes," said the king, "to the sky."

"The *sky?*" And they pointed upwards. There was the sky, as far away as anything you could think of. "You can't mean the sky," they said.

"I *do* mean the sky," said the king. And he said if all the carpenters in his kingdom didn't start work at once, he'd call for all the executioners in his kingdom. There wouldn't be a carpenter left anywhere with a head on his shoulders.

So the carpenters, who didn't like the idea of having no heads on their shoulders, went off to buy wood. They bought huge quantities of wood, and they made measurements, and they bit their lips, and I'm afraid some of them bit their fingernails. But they couldn't see how you could make a wooden tower reaching to the sky.

The king became very cross. He wanted to walk on the moon by next Saturday, at the latest. So he called the carpenters together *and* he called for his executioners, too.

"This is your last chance," he told the carpenters. "Start work tomorrow, or your heads will roll!"

So the carpenters, who didn't like the idea of their heads rolling, went away to think again. And they thought, and they thought, and they came up with an idea. They went back to the king and said they knew how to do it. But when it was finished it might be a rather dangerous tower to climb, so perhaps they should climb it first.

"Never!" cried the king. "Never! I'm not having a lot of carpenters reaching the moon before the king does. *I'll* do the climbing. You get on with the building. How do you mean to do it?"

And the carpenters told him of their plan. And he sent out all the heralds

92

in his kingdom with a message to all the men, women and children in his kingdom that they were to bring to the palace every box they had, and all the boxes would be heaped on top of one another in the palace gardens. And at last the tower of boxes was bound to reach the sky.

Well, it didn't. It was wonderfully high, and wonderfully shaky, but it didn't reach the sky. So the king ordered all the trees in his kingdom to be chopped down by all the woodcutters in his kingdom; and then all the boxmakers in his kingdom were ordered to turn the wood into boxes. When these boxes were added to the tower – well, you couldn't see the top of it. It was hidden in the clouds.

So the king started his climb. Up he went, up and up, and to the people on the ground he grew smaller and smaller. For a long time they could see his gold crown twinkling, but then they could no longer see that. For a long time they could see his silver

shoes flashing, but then they could no longer see those. The clouds swallowed him up.

Then at last, out of the clouds, came a very small, very distant voice. They cupped their ears with their hands and one or two of them, who had especially good hearing, could just make out the king's words.

"I'm nearly there," he was crying. "I just want *one more box!*"

But there wasn't a box left in the kingdom. There wasn't a tree left. There wasn't a splinter of wood, anywhere. And when they shouted this news up to the king, all the people in his kingdom shouting at once so he could hear the message travelling miles up through the air, he became *very* angry. And they heard his voice again.

"All right," he said. "*All right!*" What they must do, then, was to pull a box out from the bottom of the pile and send it up to him. That way he'd reach the moon.

Well, you can see what was wrong with that idea. Even the babies in his kingdom could see what was wrong with that. But if you'd rather have your head on than off, you don't disobey a king. So they did as they were ordered.

They pulled a box out from the bottom of the pile.

And the tower collapsed. The king came spinning out of the clouds. He came down much faster than he went up. And his crown dropped off as he fell and came twinkling through the air ahead of him.

I'll tell you one thing. It cured the king of wanting to walk on the moon.

PUNCHINELLO
KEPT A CAT

Jean Chapman

Punchinello was not only the funniest clown in all the circus, he was the happiest.

He lived in a little yellow caravan that had wheels as bright as spinning-tops. In the caravan lived Punchinello's little friend, a little grey cat called Tillica.

All the circus people liked Punchinello. All the circus people liked Tillica; that is, everyone except the Ringmaster.

The Ringmaster had a big bellowing voice. As he walked past the yellow caravan, he roared as loud as the lions. "Punchinello! Punchinello!"

Hearing that voice Punchinello put his hands over his ears to keep out some of the roar. And hearing that voice Tillica hid under the bedspread.

"Punchinello!" shouted the Ringmaster. "I hear you have a cat. We can't have a cat in this circus."

"But why?" asked Punchinello, poking his head out through the window. "Tillica is a very nice cat."

"We can't keep a cat in the circus, because people don't want to see a cat," the Ringmaster told him. "A cat can't do tricks like a bear or a monkey."

Of course Punchinello didn't want to send his little Tillica away. He tried to teach her to do tricks like the circus dogs. But all Tillica did was rub her smooth head against his baggy trousers.

The fat man who trained the seal to balance a ball on the tip of his nose came and tried to teach Tillica to balance a ball on the tip of *her* nose. But all Tillica did was to chase the ball and push it with her little white paw.

The thin man who taught the lions to sit still on their boxes came and tried to teach Tillica to stand on her hind legs and dance. But all Tillica would do was walk on her four paws with her tail in the air.

The little man who taught the elephants to walk in a circle, holding each other's tails with their trunks, tried to teach Tillica to jump through a paper hoop. But Tillica just licked her paw with a pink tongue and washed her face.

"Too bad," they all sighed to Punchinello. "Tillica can't do tricks. She's just an ordinary little grey cat."

But Punchinello had thought of an idea.

At the next performance of the circus, he didn't run into the ring with the red pompons on his cap a-bobbing and his long flat feet a-flapping. Instead he staggered in under the biggest basket ever made.

"Whatever is in that basket?" shouted the Ringmaster.

"Lift up the lid and see," Punchinello told him.

The Ringmaster opened the lid and pulled out another basket that was just a little bit smaller. "What's in this basket?" he asked.

"Look and see!" said Punchinello.

The Ringmaster found another basket inside, then another and another. Soon there were baskets all over the circus-ring. By now the children were standing in their seats and craning their necks to see what could be in the basket.

Then there came a basket that wasn't very big and it wasn't very high. The Ringmaster lifted the lid – inside sat Tillica, cleaning her whiskers!

"Oooooooooh!" said the children with mouths as round as oranges. "Do it again! Do it again!"

So, instead of frowning, the Ringmaster beamed a smile from ear to ear.

As a matter of fact, soon he was thinking it had been his idea to let Tillica surprise the children in this wonderful game.

And so Punchinello kept his cat.

THE BEST THING
TO DO

An Indian tale

Там here was once a goat, a very old goat. When the
flock made their way home from the field, she was
always the last to arrive. And one evening she was so
slow that when night fell, she was still some way from the
village. But there, on a hillside, she saw a cave. The best
thing to do, surely, was to spend the night in the cave.

And it would have been the best thing to do, except
that the cave was the den of a particularly fierce lion.

Too late, the goat smelt him. There was a strong,
yellow smell of *lion*! And too late, she caught sight of
him. He was standing just inside the entrance to the
cave, and it was obvious that *he'd* smelt *her*. And seen
her, too. He was ready to spring.

Oh dear, thought the goat. The best thing to do,
surely, was to walk straight up to him as though she
wouldn't give a blade of grass for his great yellow
shoulders, and his long yellow hair, and his terrible eyes.

And that *was* the best thing to do, because the lion
had never seen an animal come boldly up to him like

that. He'd certainly never seen an animal march straight into his cave. So instead of springing, he roared,

"Who are you, and what do you want?"

"I am the Queen of the Goats," she said. "I haven't long to live, and I've promised myself that before I die I'll eat a hundred tigers, fifty elephants and twenty-five lions. I've already eaten the hundred tigers and fifty elephants. Now I'm starting on the lions."

The lion was scared out of his wits. Please, *please*, he cried (it wasn't a word he often used), she must allow him to wash himself in the river first. If he was to die, he must die clean. And the goat thought the best thing to do was to let him go. Then she'd have the cave to herself for the night.

Well, it would have been the best thing to do, except that as he ran away from the cave the lion met a jackal. The jackal was astonished. A frightened lion! What was the world coming to? And he asked the lion what had made his yellow hair stand on end like that.

"It was horrible, *horrible!*" cried the lion, his great body still trembling. "There I was in my cave, and along came this creature! Looked like a goat, said she was their queen – but you never saw such eyes, so *green*, and such large horns, so *sharp*, and such a long beard, so terribly *white!* And she was looking for lions to eat! And she meant to start with *me.*"

The jackal smiled.

"Sounds like any old plain goat to me," he said. "Never heard of the goats having a queen, anyway. I tell you what – I'll come back to the cave with you, and if I've guessed right, we'll have a good meal tonight, you and I."

So the lion stopped shivering, and the two of them made their way back to the cave. The goat, who was just settling down for the night, smelt them coming. And then she *saw* them coming!

The best thing to do, she thought, was to brave it out.

And that was the best thing to do, as you'll see.

She marched up to the pair of them and cried,

"Oh, Master Jackal, there'll be trouble for you! Very serious trouble! I told you to bring me twenty-five lions – and what's this? You've brought me just one wretched miserable lion! I shall eat you both for this!"

I don't know what the jackal thought, but I do know what the lion thought. He thought the jackal had

cheated him. The goat had told him to bring the lion to be eaten! With the hugest of roars, he sprang at the jackal, who took to his heels. And while one was chasing the other (and I'm afraid the odds were against the jackal), the goat thought the best thing to do was to slip out of the cave and run home.

And that *was* the best thing to do!

THINGS
ARE
PUZZLING

James Reeves

Alittle girl was walking along a footpath through a field, when she happened to meet an elephant.

"What is your name?" asked the elephant.

"Cristina," said the little girl.

"You are very small," said the elephant.

"Yes, I am a small little girl."

"Goodbye," said the elephant.

The next thing Cristina happened to meet was a mouse.

"What are you?" asked the mouse.

"I am a small little girl," said Cristina.

"You are very big," said the mouse.

"Goodbye," said Cristina, as she walked on.

The next thing she happened to meet was a giraffe.

"Hallo," said the giraffe. "What are you?"

"I am a big small little girl," said Cristina.

"You are very short," said the giraffe, bending his neck down so as to look at her closer.

Cristina said goodbye and walked on. The next thing she happened to meet on the smooth footpath was a very round and prickly hedgehog.

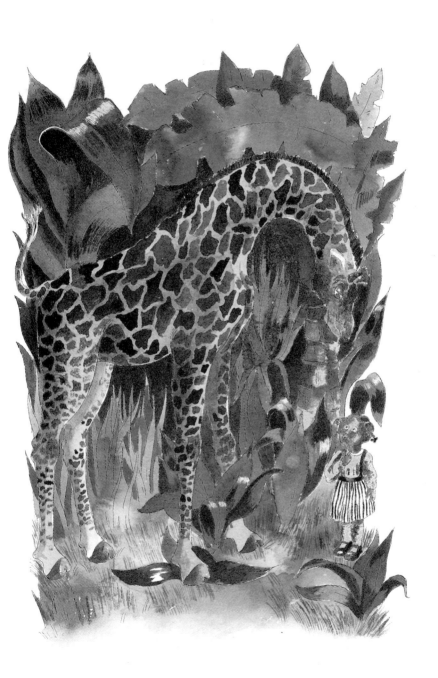

He stopped and looked up at Cristina.

"What are you?" he asked.

"I am a short big small little girl."

"You are very tall," said the hedgehog decidedly and trotted off before Cristina could say goodbye.

The next animal she happened to meet was a snake. She was not at all frightened, because she had never seen a snake before. But it ought to be mentioned that it is wise to be frightened of snakes until you have been introduced.

"What are you?" asked the snake.

"I am a tall short big small little girl," answered Cristina.

"You are very fat," said the snake.

"Goodbye," said Cristina, as the snake rippled off amongst the grass.

The next animal she happened to meet was a pig – a huge overgrown pig, grunting loudly.

"What are you?" he asked.

"I am a fat tall short big small little girl."

"You are *very* thin," said the pig, grunting.

"Goodbye," said Cristina.

The next animal she saw was a bird. It skimmed out of the sky and perched on a branch over the footpath.

"What are you?" asked the bird.

"I am a thin fat tall short big small little girl," answered Cristina, who was beginning to get tired of being so many different things.

"Well, you are very slow," said the bird, chirping. "While you have been walking across this small field, I have flown three times round the world."

But he was lying. He had only been round it once.

"Goodbye," said Cristina, leaving the bird to rest on the branch.

The next animal she happened to meet was a tortoise.

"What are you?" asked the tortoise, rather out of breath from trying to hurry.

"I am a slow thin fat tall short big small little girl. *And* I know what you're going to say next. You are going to say that I am very quick."

"I wasn't," said the tortoise decidedly in his dry, scratchy voice. "I forget *what* I was going to say. You have put it out of my head."

"Well, perhaps you can tell me," Cristina went on, "why it is that I am called so many different things."

"Things are very puzzling," answered the tortoise. "It depends how you *feel*, not what people say. Take me, for instance. They call me slow, but I often feel quite quick. When I go for a walk with my grandfather, who is a hundred and seventy-three years old, he says I am far too quick for him. Goodbye for now."

Cristina decided to go home and have tea. That at least was not puzzling.

THE
ELEPHANT
PARTY

Paul Biegel

The circus was coming! All the cars had to stop, and no one was allowed to cross the road any more, because the circus would be coming right down the middle of the street.

'Tarantara!' Twelve men tooted the music on their copper oompah-pas, which glittered in the sunshine.

'Boom! Boom! Boom!' The big drum followed behind. It was almost impossible to see the man who was beating the big drum, because the drum was ten times as big as his tummy.

And the clowns! They did not walk, they ran and skipped and danced and hopped and pulled funny faces at Mrs Keepoff de Grasse.

Behind the clowns walked the lion-tamer, with two savage lions, but they were firmly attached to a chain and walked along as demurely as puppy-dogs.

There were horses, too, and caravan after caravan after caravan. The parade took at least an hour to pass by.

"Hurrah!" cried all the children in the street. "Hurrah for the circus!"

"But there aren't any elephants," cried a little girl. She was very fond of elephants.

"There! There!" shouted her little brother. "There's one coming now!"

And lo and behold, right at the back, last of all in the long procession, came a great big grey jumbo. But how oddly he moved! So jerkily, so flabbily, so . . . so . . .

110

Then all the children shouted, "It's not real! It's not a real elephant! It's an elephant on wheels!"

They had never seen anything so funny. An elephant which looked like a toy elephant, but was as big as a real one! What could it mean? The procession stopped in the middle of the square, the caravans forming a big circle. The tent was put up and the elephant came to a stop beside it. The children were allowed to come quite close. He was big, he was very big!

"Ladies and Gentlemen!" cried the Ringmaster of the circus, who was wearing a tall hat. "Ladies and Gentlemen, this elephant is a very remarkable beast. If you will all help, you will find out just how remarkable it is. Will you all help?"

"Yeees!" shouted everybody, for everybody had come to look. There must have been about a thousand people in the square.

"Listen!" said the Ringmaster. "All the mothers must go home and cook a big saucepan of pudding – pink pudding, raspberry pudding. And when the puddings are ready, all the mothers must come back here, to the elephant. With the saucepans of pudding."

"And then?" asked the thousand people.

"You will see!" cried the Ringmaster. And then he said something absolutely horrible. He said, "All the children must go to bed!"

"Heeey!" shouted all the children.

"Otherwise the party can't go on," said the Ringmaster. "The elephant party. It begins tomorrow morning. All the children can come then."

There was nothing else for it: the children were packed off to bed. Their mothers began to cook puddings which you could smell all over town. Raspberry puddings. They smelled pink.

After an hour people began to arrive from all sides, mothers with steaming hot pans, and fathers too, because there are a great many fathers who can cook, and aunts and grandmothers and even kind ladies who had no children at all. Every one of them had a great pan, full of hot pudding.

"This way!" called the Ringmaster.

Two ladders were propped against the elephant. By each ladder stood a clown and the clowns took the pans of pudding, climbed the ladder with them and poured them out . . . into the elephant.

There was an opening in the top of the elephant, and it was getting fuller and fuller. In the end, when the last pan of pudding had been handed up by a nervous grandmother and poured out, the elephant was stuffed – stuffed with raspberry pudding.

"Now isn't that a shame!" said the people.

"Wait a bit!" said the Ringmaster. "At eight o'clock tomorrow morning all the children – *all* the children – must come here. With a spoon!"

That was more like it! By seven o'clock they were already lined up: Charlie and Jock and Hannah and Gerry and Mike and the doctor's Till and a thousand more children, every one of them with a spoon. Some with soup spoons and one child with the biggest ladle in the kitchen.

"Where's the pudding gone?" they asked.

The grown-ups hadn't given anything away.

'Tarantara!' There was the music, and here came the clowns! And what did the clowns do? They began to peel the skin off the elephant. Rip, rip! And what was left after that?

A great big pink elephant. A wibbly wobbly elephant. A shivery shaky elephant. A pudding elephant, with a pudding tail and a pudding head and pudding feet, fatter than fat, and a pudding tum, rounder than round, oh yes, the most enormous pudding in the world. Pink, with a white cap of whipped cream on its head.

"Oooh!" shouted all the children and then the elephant party began. Ladders were run up against the pudding creature, at least ten of them, and at once the biggest boys and girls climbed up them, spoon in hand, and began to eat. From its back, from its neck, from its head, from its whipped cream cap. Smaller children

113

began at the sides and the smallest of all at the feet. Pudding, pudding and more pudding they ate, with big spoons, little spoons, teaspoons, sauce spoons and one little boy with his ladle. They ate pink raspberry pudding at eight o'clock in the morning and the whole day long. The whole day, because the elephant was so big, so very big. When the real circus began that evening in the tent, the elephant had gone. All gone.

And all the children had fat, round tummies, as fat as the music man's big drum.

THE TALE OF
MR AND MRS PEPPERCORN
AND THEIR
CUCKOO-CLOCK

Elizabeth Clark

J ust in case you have never seen a cuckoo-clock I had better explain what it is before the story begins.

A cuckoo-clock is shaped like a little house made out of wood, with a pointed roof. Just under the point of the roof there is a tiny door. Under the door is a clock-face. Some clocks have a little bell that strikes 'ting-ting' to tell the hour; but a cuckoo-clock has a cuckoo. He is carved in wood and he lives just inside the tiny door. Every hour when the long hand of the clock reaches XII the door clicks open and out pops the cuckoo. 'Cuckoo!' he says, and you count the cuckoo calls and you know what time it is.

And now I will tell you the story of Mr and Mrs Peppercorn and their cuckoo-clock.

Mr and Mrs Peppercorn lived on a little farm high up on a green hillside. Mrs Peppercorn was large and stout; Mr Peppercorn was small and thin. They had a little white house and a cat and a dog. They had two brown cows and a pig and a little grey donkey. They had a cock and some speckly hens and four ducks on a tiny pond. They were as busy and as happy as the day was long. Only sometimes in spring Mrs Peppercorn said to herself, "I should like to be down in the woods to hear the cuckoo calling this fine sunshiny day, like I did when I was a little girl." But she was too busy to go down, and she was very happy with Mr Peppercorn, so she did not think about the cuckoo very often.

It was a fine sunshiny day in June when this story happened. It was early in the morning and Mr Peppercorn had on his best clothes because he was going down the hillside with the little grey donkey to the town in the valley. He was taking butter and cheese and two big baskets of eggs to sell, and he was going to bring back tea and sugar and currants and flour and other things that Mrs Peppercorn needed. And besides all these he was going to bring back a present for Mrs Peppercorn. She did not know it, but he had been saving for that present for a very long time, and now he had five silver shillings in his pocket. He did not quite know what he was going to buy, but he felt sure it would

be something very nice. So he went whistling down the hillside, and Mrs Peppercorn called after him, "Don't you hurry back, my dear; take a bit of a holiday and enjoy yourself. And be sure you listen and tell me if you hear a cuckoo calling!"

Mr Peppercorn and the donkey went happily down the green hillside and through the green woods till they came to the town. They got there just as the shops were opening, and Mr Peppercorn soon sold all his eggs and butter and cheese. Then he bought the things that Mrs Peppercorn needed, and then he began to think about buying her present. But he could not make up his mind what he should buy. He thought of a new dress. "But it might be the wrong size," he said. He thought of a new hat. "But it might be the wrong colour." He thought of a silver brooch. "But she has one already and she won't want another." He thought of all kinds of things, but none of them seemed quite right.

He was beginning to feel very puzzled and muddled when he heard a great shouting and he saw a large fat man running after a small thin dog. The small thin dog had a very large bone and the large fat man had a very big stick. The dog was so frightened that it did not see where it was going. It ran straight up the road, and suddenly it turned and before Mr Pepper-corn knew what was happening it ran between his feet. And down on his nose fell Mr Peppercorn, all mixed up with the dog and the bone, and the

big man rushed up and stood over them with the big thick stick.

Everyone was laughing except the large fat man. He looked so cross that Mr Peppercorn felt sorry for the dog. He sat up and said, "Please don't beat him."

And the man said, "I *will* beat him. He's stolen the bone that my wife was going to make soup with. I'll beat him well and tie him up. He won't have a chance to steal any more."

Mr Peppercorn felt still more sorry for the dog. He forgot all about Mrs Peppercorn's present. He only remembered that he had five silver shillings in his pocket and he said, "Don't do that. I'll buy the dog. I'll give you five shillings for him."

The fat man said in a great hurry, "You can have him," and Mr Peppercorn, who was still sitting on the ground, felt in his pocket and gave him his five precious silver shillings.

The fat man went away very pleased, and Mr Peppercorn got up rather slowly and looked at the donkey. The donkey was looking rather surprised and, to tell the truth, Mr Peppercorn was surprised too. He knew he did not want another dog, and he did not suppose Mrs Peppercorn would want one either, and

he was quite sure that Sammy, their old black dog, would not be at all pleased to see the little dog if he took it home. He did not know what to do.

He took the donkey to a stable and left him there munching hay, and then he walked a little way out of town and sat down under a tree to eat his dinner and think. His dinner was tied up in a large handkerchief. It was bread and bacon and cheese, with some radishes to munch. The small thin dog shared it with him, and it seemed so hungry that Mr Peppercorn did not have much besides radishes for his dinner that day. He gave all the rest to the dog. When it was all eaten, they walked on a little farther.

Mr Peppercorn was still thinking what to do when they came to a cottage with a garden full of flowers. Mr Peppercorn knocked at the door. He wanted a drink of water for himself and some for the little dog.

An old woman came to the door, and when Mr Peppercorn said, "Could I have some water for myself and the dog, if you please?" she said, "Come in and sit down. I'll get you some and welcome."

Mr Peppercorn sat down, and when the water came the little dog lapped up a saucerful very quickly and curled himself up on the mat by the hearth as if he had lived there all his life. Mr Peppercorn drank his water slowly, and while he drank he told the old woman about his adventure with the large fat man and how he had spent all his money on the small thin dog. "And now I don't know what to do with him," he said.

The old woman sat listening, and when he had finished she sat there thinking and presently she nodded her head.

"He's a nice little dog," she said, "and if he was well fed he wouldn't steal. Give him to me; he'll be company for me, and I'll give you a pair of white rabbits for your wife."

Mr Peppercorn thought that was a splendid idea. They went into the back garden; there were rows of carrots and lettuces and onions and potatoes and cabbages, and there was a big hutch with a whole family of fluffy white rabbits. Mr Peppercorn chose two. The old woman put them in an old basket with some hay and a carrot to nibble. She tied down the lid, and Mr Peppercorn thanked her and took the basket. He went away down the road, happy and contented with his present for Mrs Peppercorn, and the old woman and the little dog looked happy and contented too. It all seemed as nice as could be.

There was plenty of time so he did not hurry; he sat down to rest under a tree. Presently a small boy came by with a long wooden cage in his hand, and as he came nearer Mr Peppercorn could see that there was a squirrel in the cage – a little brown squirrel from the woods. The boy looked happy but the squirrel did not. It sat in the cage all bunched up and miserable, and Mr Peppercorn said to himself, "Oh dear! Oh dear! A squirrel in a cage!" And he said to the small boy, "What are you going to do with the squirrel?"

The small boy said, "Keep him in the cage for a pet."

And Mr Peppercorn forgot all about Mrs Peppercorn's present. He only thought about a squirrel shut up in a cage when it ought to be racing up and down the trees in the wood among green leaves and swinging, swaying branches.

He said, "Wouldn't you like two beautiful rabbits instead? Give the squirrel to me and you can have them." And he opened the basket a little and let the small boy peep in.

The small boy looked and he said, "O-oo-oh! *White* rabbits! You can have the squirrel!"

Mr Peppercorn gave him the basket and took the cage. The boy trotted off very happy and contented, and left Mr Peppercorn standing under the tree, considering. You know, of course, what he meant to do. He was going to let the squirrel go, as quickly as possible. He was only thinking where he could take it, and presently he trudged up the road again and turned into a little lane that ran between green hedges till it came to the edge of a wood. Mr Peppercorn stepped in among the trees and put the cage on the ground under a great beech-tree. Then he opened the door and stood back a little and watched.

The squirrel had been so frightened that it sat quite still for a minute and did not even seem to see the open door. Then suddenly it seemed to wake and it was out, running like a little red-brown streak across the rustling brown beech leaves and over mossy green roots to the big

smooth grey trunk of the tree. Up the tree it went so
nimbly, so lightly, so happily, with its tail fluffed out like
a feather and its bright eyes shining. It stopped for a
second where a big branch joined the trunk and looked
down at Mr Peppercorn as if it was saying, "Thank you
and goodbye!" Then it went on, higher and higher, up
and up, among the clear green leaves and the silver-grey
branches till it was out of sight.

Mr Peppercorn stood watching till the squirrel had
gone. Then he stooped and picked up the cage; and
suddenly he remembered that he had no present for Mrs
Peppercorn. There he was with no money in his pocket

and an empty squirrel cage in his hand. He did not want the cage, and he did not want anyone else to have it, in case they should put another squirrel in it. He could not see what to do with it.

He was walking down the lane thinking what to do, when he heard the creaking of wheels. Round the corner came a yellow caravan drawn by an old white horse. On the step of the caravan sat an old man with a rosy face and a grey beard. He looked a nice old man, but when he saw Mr Peppercorn with the squirrel cage his face grew very cross.

"What are you doing with that squirrel cage?" he called grumpily. "Nobody has any business to put a squirrel in a cage – no, they haven't," said the old man.

"I was just wondering what to do with it," said Mr Peppercorn; and he told the old man about the squirrel and how he had set it free.

The old man smiled all over his face. His eyes twinkled and he grew rosier than ever with pleasure.

"I'll tell you what we'll do," he said. "I was just wanting a nice bit of dry wood to light my fire. All the sticks in the wood are damp after last night's rain. We'll make a fire with that cage and have a cup of tea."

Mr Peppercorn was delighted. The old man got down from the caravan. They broke up the cage and lit a fire, and while the kettle boiled Mr Peppercorn told the old man all about his day's marketing and how hard he had tried to buy a present for Mrs Peppercorn. "And here I am," he said, rather sadly, "with nothing to take back to her, after all."

"Well," said the old man, "that was a nice cup of tea, wasn't it? – (Mr Peppercorn said, "Thank you.") – I am very much obliged to you for giving me such a nice bit of dry wood to make my fire with. And now," he said, "I am going to give you a present to take back to your wife. I am going to give you a clock. My grandmother had three clocks and I have them all. Three clocks are too many for one caravan. Come inside and see."

Mr Peppercorn went up the steps and in at the door and into the caravan. I wish I had time to tell you how nice it was, with its gay little window curtains and its shining paint and bright saucepans and china. But I can only tell you about the clocks. There were three of them, as the old man had said. One had a face like a moon – round and white with black numbers on it. One was large and long, in a wooden case with a coloured picture painted above the clock face and a solemn tick-tock-tick. The third clock sat on a little shelf in a corner and was quite quiet because it was not wound up. It looked like a little wooden house – a dear little brown house with a painted roof with wide edges carved into a pattern. Just under the roof was a little door like the doors you sometimes see in barns and stables. Below the little door was a clock face with white carved numbers and white carved hands.

Mr Peppercorn looked at the third clock and he thought it was lovely, and when the old man said, "That's the clock for you," his heart beat quite fast with happiness.

"That's the clock," said the old man, and he took down the clock and unscrewed the little shelf and wrapped them up in a clean piece of potato sack and gave them to Mr Peppercorn.

"Here's the key," he said, and his eyes twinkled. "You'll get a surprise when you've wound that clock."

Mr Peppercorn thanked him again and again, and trudged away down the road. His heart was filled with joy because he really had a present for Mrs Peppercorn. He turned several times to wave to the yellow caravan, and then he hurried down the hill and back to the town to get the donkey and the parcels. He packed his baskets carefully and put the clock in one of them, and then he and the donkey set out for home. Up through the woods they went and over the green hillside till they came to the little farm.

Mrs Peppercorn was standing at the gate watching for them. "Well, my dear," she said to Mr Peppercorn, "did you have a nice day and did you hear a cuckoo calling?"

"No," said Mr Peppercorn. "I didn't hear a cuckoo calling, but I had a wonderful day and I've brought you a present, my dear."

He unwrapped the clock and showed it to her, and Mrs Peppercorn was as surprised and as pleased as could be.

They put the donkey in the field to get his supper; and while Mrs Peppercorn bustled about the kitchen, Mr Peppercorn got his tools and he fixed up the little shelf for the clock. While he worked he told Mrs Peppercorn about his adventures, and she could hardly set the table for listening.

Then he wound the clock and put it in its place. It was just above the kitchen table, and as they sat at supper they could watch the white carved hand creeping from minute to minute and from one white number to another, while the short hand moved slowly till it was almost at six o'clock.

Suddenly Mr Peppercorn thought of something. "The old man said there would be a surprise," he said. "I wonder what it can be?" And just as he said it, the surprise came. You have guessed, of course, but Mr and Mrs Peppercorn had not – and it certainly was a surprise!

The long hand of the clock touched XII and the short hand touched VI. There was a click as the little door above the clock face flew open and there stood a tiny bird beautifully carved in wood. It bobbed its head and flapped its wings and opened its little bill. "Cuckoo," said the little bird clearly and sweetly, "cuckoo, cuckoo, cuckoo, cuckoo, cuckoo!" Then the little door shut with a snap and the bird was gone.

Mr and Mrs Peppercorn sat staring at the clock, too surprised to move or speak. They could hardly believe it was real. Mrs Peppercorn pinched herself and poked Mr Peppercorn to make certain that it was not a dream. "If it happens again at seven o'clock, I shall know it's true," she said.

And, of course, as you know, it did. The cuckoo popped out at seven o'clock and again at eight. They heard it faintly in the night and when they got down in the morning it was all ready to call 'Cuckoo!' seven times when they sat down to their breakfast at seven o'clock.

They soon got used to it and they always loved it. They even left the kitchen door open at night so that they could hear the cuckoo calling in the dark. "It's easy to get up, even on a winter's morning, with that to call you," said Mrs Peppercorn, and she was not sorry any more that she could not go down the hill to hear the cuckoo in the woods in spring.

"Now we have a cuckoo-clock," she often said cheerfully to Mr Peppercorn, "it's spring-time in the house all the year round."

And Mr Peppercorn smiled happily at her and thought how lucky he was to have Mrs Peppercorn – and a cuckoo-clock into the bargain!

THE STAMPING ELEPHANT

Anita Hewett

E lephant stamped about in the jungle, thumping down his great grey feet on the grass and the flowers and the small soft animals.

He squashed the tiny shiny creatures and trod on the tails of the creeping creatures. He beat down the corn seedlings, crushed the lilacs, and stamped on the morning glory flowers.

"We must stop all this stamping," said Goat, Snake and Mouse.

Goat said, "Yes, we must stop it. But *you* can't do anything, Mouse."

And Snake said, "Of course she can't. Oh no, *you* can't do anything, Mouse."

Mouse said nothing. She sat on the grass and listened while Goat told his plan.

"Scare him, that's what I'll do," said Goat. "Oh good, good, good, I'll scare old Elephant, frighten him out of his wits, I will."

He found an empty turtle shell and hung it up on a low branch. Then he beat on the shell with his horns.

"This is my elephant-scaring drum. I shall beat it, clatter, clatter," he said. "Elephant will run away. Oh good, good, good."

Stamp, stamp, stamp. Along came Elephant.

Goat tossed his head and ran at the shell, clatter, clatter, beating it with his horns.

"Oh, what a clatter I'm making," he bleated. "Oh, what a terrible, elephant-scaring, horrible clatter."

Elephant said, *"What* a nasty little noise!"

He took the shell in his long trunk, lifted it high up into the air, and banged it down on Goat's hairy head. Then he went on his way, stamping.

Mouse said nothing. But she thought, "Poor old Goat looks sad, standing there with a shell on his head." Then she sat down on the grass and listened while Snake told his plan.

"I shall make myself into a rope," said Snake. "Yes, yes, yes, that's what I'll do." He looped his body around a tree trunk. "Now I'm an elephant-catching rope. Yes, yes, yes, that's what I am. I shall hold old Elephant tight by the leg, and I shan't let him go. No, I shan't let him go, till he promises not to stamp any more."

Stamp, stamp, stamp. Along came Elephant.

Snake hid in the long grass. Elephant stopped beside a tree, propped up his two white tusks on a branch, and settled himself for a nice little sleep.

Snake came gliding out of the grass. He looped his long body around the tree trunk and around old Elephant's leg as well. His teeth met his tail at the end of the loop, and he bit on his tail tip, holding fast.

"I have looped old Elephant's leg to the tree trunk. Now I must hold on tight," he thought.

Elephant woke, and tried to move. But with only three legs he was helpless.

"Why are you holding my leg?" he shouted.

Snake kept quiet. He could not speak. If he opened his mouth the loop would break.

Elephant put his trunk to the ground and filled it with tickling, yellow dust. Then he snorted, and blew the dust at Snake.

Snake wriggled. He wanted to sneeze.

Elephant put his trunk to the ground and sniffed up more of the tickling dust. "Poof!" he said, and he blew it at Snake.

Snake held his breath and wriggled and squirmed, trying his hardest not to sneeze. But the dust was too tickly. "Ah ah ah!" He closed his eyes and opened his mouth. "Ah ah tishoo!" The loop was broken.

Elephant said, "*What* a nasty little cold!"

And he went on his way, stamping.

Mouse said nothing. But she thought, "Snake looks sad, lying there sneezing his head off." Then she sat on the grass and made her own plan.

Stamp, stamp, stamp. Along came Elephant.

Mouse peeped out of her hole and watched him. He lay

on his side, stretched out his legs, and settled himself for a nice long sleep.

Mouse breathed deeply, and stiffened her whiskers. She waited till Elephant closed his eyes. Then she crept through the grass like a little grey shadow, her bright brown eyes watching Elephant's trunk. She made her way slowly around his great feet, and tiptoed past his shining tusks. She trotted along by his leathery trunk until she was close to its tender pink tip. Then suddenly, skip! she darted backwards, and sat in the end of Elephant's trunk.

Elephant opened his eyes, and said, "Can't I have *any* peace in this jungle? First it's a silly clattering goat, then it's a sillier sneezing snake, and now it's a mouse, the smallest of them all, and quite the silliest. That's what *I* think."

He looked down his long grey trunk and said, "Oh yes, I know you are there, little mouse, because I can see your nose and whiskers. Out you get! Do you hear, little mouse?"

"Eek," said Mouse, "I won't get out, unless you promise not to stamp."

"Then I'll shake you out," Elephant shouted, and he swung his trunk from side to side.

"Thank you," squeaked Mouse, "I'm having a ride. It's almost like flying. Thank you, Elephant."

Elephant shouted, "I'll drown you out." He stamped to the river and waded in, dipping the end of his trunk in the water.

"Thank you," squeaked Mouse, "I'm having a swim. It's almost like diving. Thank you, Elephant."

135

Elephant stood on the bank, thinking. He could not pull down the leaves for his dinner. He could not give himself a bath. He could not live, with a mouse in his trunk.

"Please, little mouse, get out of my trunk. Please," he said.

"Will you promise not to stamp?" asked Mouse.

"No," said Elephant.

"Then this is what I shall do," said Mouse, and she tickled his trunk with her tail.

"Now will you promise not to stamp?"

"No," said Elephant.

"Then this is what I shall do," said Mouse and she nipped his trunk with her sharp little teeth.

"Yes," squealed Elephant. "Yes, yes, yes."

Mouse ran back to her hole and waited.

Step, step, step. Along came Elephant, walking gently on great grey feet. He saw the tiny shiny creatures, and waited until they scuttled away. He saw the little creeping creatures, and stepped very carefully over their tails.

"Elephant doesn't stamp any more. *Someone* has stopped him," the creatures said. "Someone big and brave and clever."

Goat said, "I think Mouse did it."

And Snake said, "Oh yes, that is right, Mouse did it."

And not far away, at the foot of a tree, a small, contented, tired little mouse sat on the grass and smiled to herself.

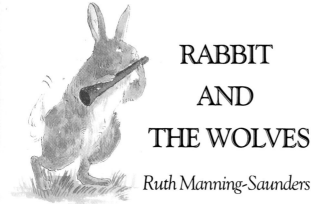

RABBIT
AND
THE WOLVES

Ruth Manning-Saunders

Rabbit's grandmother had given him a little pipe. Now he was skipping along through the woods, *lipperty-lipperty-lip-lip-lipperty*, and playing on his little pipe. Rabbit didn't live in the woods himself. He lived in Grandmother's house; but he had lots of friends in the woods, and his best friend of all was Marmot, who lived in a hole under a tree stump. Now Rabbit was going to show his new pipe to Marmot. He was looking forward to showing the pipe to his best friend, Marmot.

So on frisked Rabbit, *lipperty-lipperty-lip-lip-lipperty* . . . and then, oh dear, what do you think? Out from behind the trees jumped seven great wolves.

"Rabbit, we're going to eat you!"

Rabbit was a brave little fellow. If he was frightened, he wasn't going to show it. He said, "Well, I own you've caught me fairly. But, dear me, you can't *all* eat me, you know; I'm only a mouthful. Well, which of you is it to be?"

The Wolves began to quarrel then, because they all wanted to eat Rabbit. But Rabbit said, "Don't quarrel! Don't quarrel! I've got a good idea. Do you like dancing?"

"Of course we do! Of course we do!" cried the Wolves.

"Well then," said Rabbit, "I know a lovely new dance, and I was just longing to teach it to someone. Shall I teach it to you? Then the one who dances best can have me for a prize."

The Wolves agreed that it *was* a good idea. So Rabbit said, "This dance is in seven parts. For the first part, you get into line, one behind the other. I lean against this tree, and when I begin to sing, you all dance away from me. When I stop singing and call out '*Hu!*' then you dance back. But you must keep in line, and dance properly; no floundering about."

"No, no! No floundering about!" cried the Wolves.

So Rabbit leaned against a tree and began to sing:

> "*Ha, how tasty,*
> *Ha, how toothsome,*
> *Ha, how tender,*
> *Little Rabbit flesh!*"

And the Wolves danced away from him, keeping in line, one behind the other, and lifting their feet to the time of his singing.

"*Hu!*" cried Rabbit, when they had danced some way. And the Wolves swung round and came dancing back to him. "Keep in line, keep in line!" cried Rabbit. "Lift your feet neatly! Ah, that's very good . . . Yes, that was really charming!" he said, as the Wolves gathered round him.

"Now," said he, "we come to the second part of the dance. I go to that tree over there, and you form in line again. I sing, you dance away, and when I call '*Hu!*' you turn and come dancing back. This second part of the dance is very like the first, only at every fourth step you fling back your heads and give a nice little howl. Got that?"

"Yes, yes," cried the Wolves. "This is great fun!"

So Rabbit went and leaned against this other tree, and began to sing again:

140

"Ha, how tasty,
Ha, how toothsome,
Ha, how tender,
Little Rabbit flesh!"

And the Wolves danced away, keeping in line, one behind the other, lifting their feet, and at every fourth step flinging back their heads and howling. It would have been the funniest sight in the world, if only Rabbit had felt more like laughing. But he didn't feel like laughing, you may be sure.

So, when the Wolves had danced quite a long way, he called out "*Hu!*" and the Wolves all turned and came dancing back.

"Well now, that was even better than the first time," said Rabbit. "In all my life I've never seen such beautiful dancing!" And he went on to a third tree. "For this third part of the dance you do a polka," said he. "Do you know the polka step?"

"Of course we do!" cried the Wolves.

"Well then, off you go!" said Rabbit. And he began to sing, "*One* and *two* and *three* and *four! Hop* and *hop* and *hop* and *hop!*"

Off went the Wolves, hopping and skipping. They were laughing like anything. They were enjoying themselves so much that they had almost forgotten about eating Rabbit. Though of course Rabbit knew they would remember it again as soon as the dance ended.

"*Hu!*" he called once more, and all the Wolves came polka-ing back. "Magnificent!" said Rabbit, moving to a fourth tree.

And what do you think cunning little Rabbit was doing, as he moved from tree to tree? Just this: with every tree he came to, he was getting nearer and nearer to the hole under the tree stump where his best friend, Marmot, lived.

So he sent the Wolves off in a fourth dance and a fifth dance, and a sixth dance, and between every dance he moved on to another tree, nearer to Marmot's hole.

"*Hu!*" he cried for the sixth time. And the Wolves came dancing back. They were really proud of themselves.

And Rabbit moved to yet another tree.

"Now this is the seventh and last part of the dance," said he. "It's called the Sun dance, and it's a gallop. You go as fast as you can, and at every seventh step you turn a somersault. Understand? Well then, get ready to go. I'll count three, and then you start. But remember as soon as I shout 'Hu!' you all turn round and come racing back. And then – oh dear! – the first that reaches me gobbles me up. . . . Well, of course," he added, wiping his eyes, "one can't live for ever. But seeing you dance so beautifully has made my last moments happy . . . One, two, *three!*" he shouted, and off galloped the Wolves.

> *"Dance away, Wolves, dance away!*
> *See us dancing, dancing, dancing!*
> *We dance, we dance, we dance the Sun dance,*
> *See how beautifully we dance!"*

sang Rabbit.

"Dance away now, dance away!" shouted the Wolves, turning a somersault at every seventh step. "See how beautifully we dance!"

"Hurrah!" cried Rabbit.

"*Hurrah! Hurrah! Hurrah!*" shouted the Wolves. Their voices were getting fainter and fainter. They were a long way off now. Rabbit could only just see their grey bodies flickering in and out among the trees. But something else he could see, quite close to him, and that was the tree stump where Marmot had her hole. And, bless me, if that wasn't Marmot's little anxious face, peeping out at him!

"*Hu!*" shouted Rabbit – and made a dash for the hole.

The Wolves turned and came racing back, each one determined to be first, that he might gobble up Rabbit. But what did they see when they came back to the starting place? Nothing at all!

Only from under the ground nearby they heard Rabbit singing:

> "Dance away now, dance away,
> Dance away, Wolves, dance away!
> But you won't eat Rabbit, not today,
> Not today, Wolves, not today!"

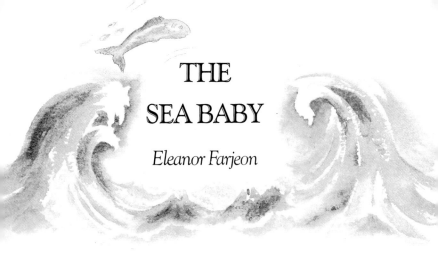

THE
SEA BABY

Eleanor Farjeon

The stocking-basket was empty. For once there was nothing to darn. The Old Nurse had told so many stories, that she had mended all the holes made by Doris and Mary Matilda, and even by Ronnie and Roley. Tomorrow they would make some more, of course, but tonight the Old Nurse sat with her hands folded in her lap, and watched the children fall asleep by fire-light.

Only one of them kept awake. Mary Matilda would not go to sleep. She was not cross, she was not ill, there was no reason at all except that she was wide awake. She kept on standing up in her cot and laughing at the Old Nurse over the bars. And when the Old Nurse came and laid her down and tucked her up, she turned over and laughed at the Old Nurse *between* the cot-bars.

"Go to sleep, Mary Matilda," said the Old Nurse in her hush-hush voice. "Shut your eyes, my darling, and go to sleep."

But Mary Matilda couldn't, or if she could, she wouldn't. And at last the Old Nurse did what she very seldom did: she came over to Mary Matilda, and took her out of the cot, and carried her to the fire, and rocked her on her knee.

"Can't you go to sleep, baby?" she crooned. "Can't you go to sleep, then? Ah, you're just my Sea-Baby over again! *She* never went to sleep, either, all the time I nursed her. And she was the very first I ever nursed. I've never told anybody about her since, but I'll tell you, Mary Matilda. So shut your eyes and listen, while I tell about my Sea-Baby."

I couldn't tell you when it happened: it was certainly a long time after the Flood, and I know I was only about ten years old, and had never left the Norfolk village on the sea-coast where I was born. My father was a fisherman, and a tiller of the land; and my mother kept the house and span the wool and linen for our clothes. But that tells us nothing, for fathers have provided the food, and mothers have kept the house, since the beginning of things. So don't go asking any more when it was that I nursed my very first baby.

It happened like this, Mary Matilda. Our cottage stood near the edge of the cliff, and at high tide the sea came right up to the foot, but at low tide it ran so far back that it seemed almost too far to follow it. People said that once, long ago, the sea had not come in so close; and that the cliff had gone out many miles farther. And on the far end of the cliff had stood another village. But after the Flood all that part of the cliff was drowned under the sea, and the village along with it. And there, said the people, the village still lay, far out to sea under the waves; and on stormy nights, they said, you could hear the church bells ringing in the church tower below the water. Ah, don't you start laughing at your old Nanny now! We knew it was true, I tell you. And one day something happened to prove it.

A big storm blew up over our part of the land; the biggest storm that any of us could remember, so big that we thought the Flood had come again. The sky was as black as night all day long, and the wind blew so hard that it drove a strong man backwards, and the rain poured down so that you only had to hold a pitcher out of the window for a second, and when you took it in it was flowing over, and the thunder growled and crackled so that we had to make signs to each other, for talking was no use, and the lightning flashed so bright that my mother could thread her needle by it. That *was* a storm, that was! My mother was frightened, but my father, who was weather-wise, watched the sky and said from time to time, "I think that'll come out all right." And so it did. The lightning and thunder flashed and rolled themselves away into the distance, the rain stopped, the wind died down, the sky cleared up for a beautiful evening, and the sun turned all the vast wet sands to a sheet of gold as far as the eye could see. Yes, and farther! For a wonder had happened during the storm. The sea had been driven back so far that it had vanished out of sight, and sands were laid bare that no living man or woman had viewed before. And there, far, far across the golden beach, lay a tiny village, shining in the setting sun.

Think of our excitement, Mary Matilda! It was the drowned village of long ago, come back to the light of day.

Everybody gathered on the shore to look at it. And suddenly I began to run towards it, and all the other children followed me. At first our parents called, "Come back! Come back! The sea may come rolling in before you can get there." But we were too eager to see the village for ourselves, and in the end the big folk felt the same about it; and they came running after the children across the sands. As we drew nearer, the little houses became plainer, looking like blocks of gold in the evening light; and the little streets appeared like golden brooks, and the church spire in the middle was like a point of fire.

For all my little legs, I was the first to reach the village. I had had a start of the others, and could always run fast as a child and never tire. We had long stopped running, of course, for the village was so far out that our breath would not last. But I was still walking rapidly when I reached the village and turned a corner. As I did so, I heard one of the big folk cry, "Oh, look! Yonder lies the sea." I glanced ahead, and did see, on the far horizon beyond the village, the shining line of the sea that had gone so far away. Then I heard another grown-up cry, "Take care! Take care! Who knows when it may begin to roll back again? We have come far, and oh, suppose the sea should overtake us before we can reach home!" Then, peeping round my corner, I saw everybody take fright and turn tail, running as hard as they could across the mile or so of sands they had just crossed. But nobody had noticed me, or thought of me; no doubt my own parents thought I was one of the band of running children, and so they left me alone there, with all the little village to myself.

What a lovely time I had, going into the houses, up and down the streets, and through the church. Everything was left as it had been, and seemed ready for someone to come to; the flowers were blooming in the gardens, the fruit was hanging on the trees, the tables were spread for the next meal, a pot was standing by the kettle on the hearth in one house, and in another there were toys upon the floor. And when I began to go upstairs to the other rooms, I found in every bed someone asleep. Grandmothers and grandfathers, mothers and fathers, young men and young women, boys and girls: all so fast asleep, that there was no waking them. And at last, in a little room at the top of a house, I found a baby in a cradle, wide awake.

She was the sweetest baby I had ever seen. Her eyes were as blue as the sea that had covered them so long, her

skin as white as the foam, and her little round head as gold as the sands in the evening sunlight. When she saw me, she sat up in her cradle, and crowed with delight. I knelt down beside her, held out my arms, and she cuddled into them with a little gleeful chuckle. I carried her about the room, dancing her up and down in my arms, calling her my baby, my pretty Sea-Baby, and showing her the things in the room and out of the window. But as we were looking out of the window at a bird's nest in a tree, I seemed to see the shining line of water on the horizon begin to move.

"The sea is coming in!" I thought. "I must hurry back before it catches us." And I flew out of the house with the Sea-Baby in my arms, and ran as hard as I could out of the village, and followed the crowd of golden footsteps on the sands, anxious to get home soon. When I had to pause to get my breath, I ventured to glance over my shoulder, and there behind me lay the little village, still glinting in the sun. On I ran again, and after a while was forced to stop a second time. Once more I glanced behind me, and this time the village was not to be seen: it had disappeared beneath the tide of the sea, which was rolling in behind me.

Then how I scampered over the rest of the way! I reached home just as the tiny wavelets, which run in front of the big waves, began to lap my ankles, and I scrambled up the cliff, with the Sea-

Baby in my arms, and got indoors, panting for breath. Nobody was at home, for as it happened they were all out looking for me. So I took my baby upstairs, and put her to bed in my own bed, and got her some warm milk. But she turned from the milk, and wouldn't drink it. She only seemed to want to laugh and play with me. So I did for a little while, and then I told her she must go to sleep. But she only laughed some more, and went on playing.

"Shut your eyes, baby," I said to her, "hush-hush! Hush-hush!" (just as my own mother said to me). But the baby didn't seem to understand, and went on laughing.

Then I said, "You're a very naughty baby" (as my mother sometimes used to say to me). But she didn't mind that either, and just went on laughing. So in the end I had to laugh too, and play with her.

My mother heard us, when she came into the house; and she ran up to find me, delighted that I was safe. What was her surprise to find the baby with me! She asked me where it had come from, and I told her; and she called my father, and he stood scratching his head, as most men do when they aren't quite sure about a thing.

"I want to keep it for my own, Mother," I said.

"Well, we can't turn it out now it's in," said my mother. "But you'll have to look after it yourself, mind."

I wanted nothing better! I'd always wanted to nurse things, whether it was a log of wood, or a kitten, or my mother's shawl rolled into a dumpy bundle. And now I had a little live baby of my own to nurse. How I did enjoy myself that week! I did everything for it; dressed and undressed it, washed it and combed its hair; and played and danced with it, and talked with it and walked with it. And I tried to give it its meals, but it wouldn't eat; and I tried to put it to sleep, but it wouldn't shut its eyes. No, not for anything I could do, though I sang to it, and rocked it, and told it little stories.

It didn't worry me much, for I knew no better: but it worried my mother, and I heard her say to my father, "There's something queer about that child. I don't know, I'm sure!"

On the seventh night after the storm, I woke up suddenly from my dreams, as I lay in bed with my baby beside me. It was very late, my parents had long gone to bed themselves, and what had wakened me I did not know, for I heard no sound at all. The moon was very bright, and filled the square of my window-pane with silver light; and through the air outside I saw something swimming – I thought at first it was a white cloud, but as it reached my open window I saw it was a lady, moving along the air as though she were swimming in water. And the strange thing was that her eyes were fast shut; so that as her white arms moved out and in she seemed to be swimming not only in the air, but in her sleep.

She swam straight through my open window to the bedside, and there she came to rest, letting her feet down upon the floor like a swimmer setting his feet on the sands under his body. The lady leaned over the bed with her shut eyes, and took my wide-awake baby in her arms.

153

"*Hush-hush! Hush-hush!*" she said; and the sound of her voice was not like my mother's voice when she said it, but like the waves washing the shore on a still night; such a peaceful sound, the sort of sound that might have been the first sound made in the world, or else the last. You couldn't help wanting to sleep as you heard her say it. I felt my head begin to nod, and as it grew heavier and heavier, I noticed that my Sea-Baby's eyelids were beginning to droop too. Before I could see any more, I fell asleep; and when I awoke in the morning my baby had gone. "Where to, Mary Matilda? Ah, you mustn't ask me that! I only know she must have gone where all babies go when they go to sleep. Go to sleep. Hush-hush! *Hush-hush! Go to sleep!*"

Mary Matilda had gone to sleep at last. The Old Nurse laid her softly in her cot, turned down the light, and crept out of the nursery.

ONE AT A TIME

A Slovenian tale

There was an old man once who had a son. One day he said to his son,

"You're a big fellow now. I think it's time you went out into the world and found some work to do."

So that's what the young man did. He travelled a long way and at last he met a farmer who wanted someone to look after his sheep. He was a very rich farmer, and it was a very large flock of sheep. The farm was spread over seven large valleys, which lay between eight large hills, and every valley and every hill was dotted with the farmer's sheep.

One day there was a storm. Not an ordinary storm but an *extra*ordinary storm! Not just thunder and lightning, but floods of rain and a mighty wind. The air was full of flying branches torn off trees. The streams were overflowing, the valleys were filling with water, and the bridges were washed away. The young man had to drive all the sheep together, from all the seven valleys and eight hills, and take them to shelter.

By the time the young man reached the farm, there was only one bridge left. It was a single plank, and the wood was old and ready to break. The sheep could go across only one at a time. The storm howled, the floods rose, and the sheep went across that shaky old plank, one at a time. One at a time. One at a time.

You want to know what happened next? I'll tell you when all the sheep have got across. They're still going over the plank, one at a time. One at a time. One at a time.

You want to know if all the sheep have got across yet? I'm afraid not. As I said, there were lots and lots of them. Well, there were all the sheep in those seven valleys and on those eight hills, added together, and now crossing the shaky old bridge, one at a time. One at a time. One at a time.

You want to know when all the sheep will have crossed over. Well, I *can* tell you that. They will all have crossed over when they are all on the other side.

But the very latest news I have is that they are still going across, one at a time.

One at a time.

One at a time.

For permission to reproduce copyright material
acknowledgement and thanks are due to the following:

J M Dent & Sons Ltd for "The Rare Spotted Birthday
Party" from *Leaf Magic* by Margaret Mahy; Little, Brown &
Co for "The Cat and the Parrot" from *Tales Told in India* by
Virginia Haviland; Methuen London Ltd for "How The
Starfish Was Born" from *Sometime Stories* by Donald Bisset;
Margaret Stuart Barry for "The Witch and the Little
Village Bus"; Methuen Children's Books for "The Cross
Photograph" from *More My Naughty Little Sister Stories* by
Dorothy Edwards; Hodder & Stoughton Ltd for "The
Donkey That Helped Father Christmas" from *Twilight and
Fireside* by Elizabeth Clark; Jonathan Cape Ltd for "The
Little Boy's Secret" from *The Book of Giant Stories* by David
L Harrison; Frank L Gilbert for "The Mermaid's Crown"
by Ruth Ainsworth; Thames Methuen for "Mother
Kangaroo" from *Rainbow Yellow Story Book* by John
Kershaw; Marie Smith for "The Toymaker's Shop"; Angus
& Robertson Ltd and the Australian Broadcasting
Commission for "Punchinello Kept a Cat" from *Listening
Time* by Jean Chapman; Blackie and Son Limited for
"Things are Puzzling" from *Egg-Time Stories* by James
Reeves; Penguin Books Ltd for "The Elephant Party" from
The Elephant Party and other stories by Paul Biegel; Hodder
& Stoughton Ltd for "The Tale of Mr and Mrs Peppercorn
and their Cuckoo-clock" from *Country Tales to Tell* by
Elizabeth Clark; The Bodley Head for "The Stamping
Elephant" from *The Anita Hewett Animal Story Book* by
Anita Hewett; Methuen Children's Books for "Rabbit and
the Wolves" from *Tortoise Tales* by Ruth Manning-Saunders;
Penguin Books Ltd for "The Sea-Baby" from *Eleanor
Farjeon's Book of Stories, Verses and Plays* by Eleanor Farjeon.